MAD MAX MURPHY

First Edition

Text set in New Baskerville
Copyright 2001 by Robert Holland
Printed on acid-free paper in Peterborough, Canada
ISBN 0 - 9658523-8-5

Cover and title page illustrations by
Kirk Roberts

Frost Hollow Publishers,LLC
411 Barlow Cemetery Road
Woodstock, CT 06281
phone: 860-974-2081
fax: 860-974-0813
email:frstholw@neca.com
website: frosthollowpub.com

"Books for boys and young men"

MAD MAX MURPHY

A Novel of Sports and Mystery

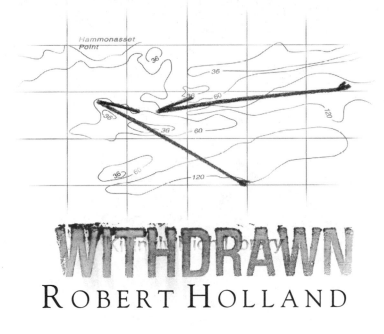

ROBERT HOLLAND

FROST HOLLOW
PUBLISHERS, LLC
Woodstock, Connecticut

More Books For
Boys And Young Men
By

Robert Holland

The Voice of the Tree
The Purple Car
Summer on Kidd's Creek
Footballs Never Bounce True
Breakin' Stones
Eben Stroud
Harry the Hook

Coming This Year:

The One-Legged Man
Who Came Out
Of A Well

Check your local bookseller or order directly from Frost Hollow. Call toll free at 877-974-2081.

All the above titles are $10.95 except for Harry The Hook, which is $11.95. Shipping and handling and sales tax extra.

Also check out our web site at frosthollowpub.com. Read about the books in the series and find out what's coming next.

One

The Boat

Mad Max Murphy saw it coming from a long way off, down by the Beach Club, in fact; a big boat, probably forty feet long, a yacht with a fly bridge over the main cabin. But what caught his eye was the great curling bow wave, and the huge roll of the wake. And while that wasn't so unusual with a boat that size, this boat had come between the rocks and the Beach Club at full throttle and there was nothing normal about that. The wake, rolling out like ocean waves, had set all the small sailboats rocking onto their beam ends, their masts whipping like the wands on energized metronomes, and you didn't have to live near Long Island Sound for long to know that there were no-wake laws around every mooring.

Max shrugged and shook his head. There was never a water cop around when you needed one. Too bad. It'd have been a hoot to see that big yacht overhauled. What nobody needed was another big-boat crazy, probably drunk and ignoring the laws because he was rich enough to afford such a big boat. Guys like that never thought the laws applied to them. It was really too bad Starchy wasn't on patrol. A pinch like this would have made his day ... especially if the guy had been drinking.

Max sat back into his beach chair and stretched his legs into the full roar of the sun. Man, he was glad summer had finally gotten here. Not only was it warm, but his days were wide open. School was out, he hadn't been able to find a job (his mother didn't want him working in the family restaurant), and all he had to think about was how well he'd play in the Shoreline Summer Soccer League, summer girls, his project, and the road part of his driving lessons. Soccer and the project he could handle but the other two ... well, not so easy. Girls were unpredictable and the driving lessons had him rattled. But no matter how you looked at it, all four had a lot to do with his future and the truth was that anything which had to do with his "future" made him as nervous as a bird on open ground.

Four things and he could fail at any one of them. And adults thought they had pressure to face. It was nothing like this. They could mess up and hardly anybody ever knew. But if he screwed up everyone knew. And then he grinned to himself, knowing that he would have it no other way. Life was a matter of taking risks. And what was he really risking here? The only one he could fail at that would be really embarrassing was not getting his license. Truly ugly. Having some girl put him down would reach an awesome level of nastiness, but, on the other hand, stuff like that happened to every guy he knew. They were always getting put down by girls of some kind, not to mention teachers. Still, try as he might, he couldn't think of any guy who hadn't gotten his license on the first shot.

The Boat

At five-eleven and a hundred and seventy-two pounds, he was a little on the large side for fifteen but he didn't think he'd grow much more. He was already an inch taller than his father and taller than any of his uncles and cousins. In fact, he was the tallest guy in his whole family, and he was easily tall enough to play in goal, especially since he had kind of long arms, not like knuckle draggers or anything, but he had to get shirts with extra long sleeves. After summer league he'd be ready to make a run at the Varsity in the fall. Preston Watkins was an okay goalie, but he locked up on penalty shots and he couldn't read the kicker well enough to cheat left or right. Every time he had to face a kick it was as if someone had nailed his feet to the ground, and by the time he reacted the ball had flown past into the net. It was hard to win when your goalie couldn't stop the tough shots.

To play in goal you had to have imagination and you had to think fast. Then you had to make your body do what you wanted. Sometimes that meant nothing more than leaping, but to stop the tough shots, the ones that got redirected close to the goal, you had to change direction or even reverse direction in a split second. There was no time to think, you either reacted or you didn't. Pure instinct. And that was what he did best. But it only worked if you kept your focus on the ball. Any break in concentration and the ball went past. And maintaining that focus was hard because most of the time you waited, watching the plays develop and keeping track of the opposing players as they moved toward the goal. It meant you had to turn it on when you needed it, to go from just watching to being the critical player on the field. Nothing could match that feeling.

He grinned as he lay with his eyes closed, picturing the

penalty shots he'd stopped in the past. It was still hard to believe he had gotten to some of them, especially the high shots in the far corners. He was getting pumped just thinking about them. There was nothing like soccer, though he supposed he felt that way because he was good at it. And he was truly good at it. Man, he ate up penalty shots the way school teachers gobbled pastries.

But for now, at ten in the morning, with practice not until one, he could work on his tan and see who turned up to hang out with. He'd brought a book with him but he wasn't much of a beach reader. Too many things to keep track of. Winter and rainy days — that's when he read books. Every Christmas he got four books and one of them was always a Dick Francis novel and for the past two years, novels by Kenneth Roberts ... a writer you could really get your teeth into. He opened his eyes and looked at the little kids playing in the water, watched closely by their bikini-clad baby sitters, girls in their twenties and most of them from Europe. Too bad they were so much older, because they sure were pretty and every one of them was put together like the girls in the Victoria's Secret catalog.

He looked out over the water at the boat. It was still a long way off, but coming steadily closer, hammering through the water at full throttle, and the bow hadn't turned. He chuckled to himself. If it held steady it would wind up in his lap.

In fact ... he stood up to get a better look. Yup. Headed right at him and everybody else who sat on the small sandy beach just inside the great stone jetty. In the breeze coming at him over the water he could hear the engines howling and he wondered what the guy could be thinking.

Off to the left lay several blubbery whalelike women

flopped out on the beach as if they had washed ashore and been stranded by the outgoing tide. Was he the only one who had noticed the boat? Should he holler? No. Things like this just didn't happen ... except that they did, and especially they happened to him. He looked out at the boat. How close would it have to get before people couldn't get out of the way? He glanced at the women with the children. They all looked like they could scamper pretty fast but the blubber balls would be real slow off the mark.

The boat showed no sign of changing course as it rushed toward them, and he tried to gauge the speed. Thirty knots, at least. He checked the position of the boat against the row of big cottages along the shoreline, glanced quickly back at the boat, and threw his arms into the air. "EVERYONE GET OFF THE BEACH!" he shouted, "GET OFF THE BEACH!"

Only the baby-sitters reacted, grabbing their wards and rushing up the narrow beach to where a solid masonry wall divided the parking lot from the sand.

Max shouted again, louder this time and slowly the heads came up, turned toward the boat, and suddenly people were screaming and running every which way as they scrambled to avoid the oncoming yacht.

The fat ones began to stir, reacting so slowly you'd have thought they'd been harpooned. "HEY!" Max shouted. "GET OFF THE BEACH!" The boat was about half a soccer field away. "GET OFF THE BEACH!" he shouted again, and finally the whales began to move with some urgency. Getting the bodies to follow was another matter. They rolled to a sitting position and then rolled again and, using their hands, began jackknifing upward. Even on their feet they could only waddle and just then the boat knifed on through a sailboat and then sliced into a big outboard as it drove past into the shallow water and the props began to scour the bottom.

That slowed the momentum some, but not enough to keep the yacht from running right up onto the beach and coming to rest with its bow just touching the wall. Now the engines were screaming and Max ran to the back of the boat, leaped up onto the swim platform, and then dashed up the ladder to the fly bridge where he jerked back on the throttles and then shut off the engines.

The quiet that followed would have challenged the silence in a math class after a big lunch. People looked stunned as they walked around, staring at the yacht, its rails some ten feet from the ground. Out in the water, the sailboat had sunk and now only the top of its mast showed. The outboard had been sliced in half and the two halves, full of flotation, were bobbing along in the gentle waves, the bow still attached to its mooring line.

He looked up as he heard the police sirens in the distance, shrugged, and climbed down to the main deck of the boat. He opened the door and stepped into the cabin, glanced around, and then quickly stepped back out and closed the door. It looked like the aftermath of a video game. No. It was a whole lot worse.

"Is there anyone in there?" one of the women called.

He nodded.

"What happened?"

Max shrugged. And then he did what cops do when faced with horror, he tried to find a way to laugh. "Kinda hard to say. It looks like he lost his head."

"Well, we know that," one of the whale women said. "Why else would he drive his boat up onto the beach?"

"Because his head's on one side of the cabin and his body's on the other." Max shook his head. "Makes it hard to see where you're going."

He could see they thought he was lying. He decided not to mention the bloody machete lying on the floor.

"You can't be serious," the whale-woman said.

"Do you think I'm making this up? Look, somebody cut the guy's head off and set the boat on autopilot."

Disbelief gave way to belief and then horror, and the crowd voted with their feet, drawing back to leave plenty of room between themselves and the boat.

The first cop there was Peter Smith's older brother Sean, and he leaped out of the cruiser, ran to the back of the boat, and climbed up onto the deck. "What happened?" he asked. "Were you on the boat, Max?"

"No. I just climbed up to shut off the engines." He nodded his head toward the cabin. "It's really ugly, Sean. Somebody cut the guy's head off."

"Whoa," Sean said, "now that is ugly." He opened the door, took one look, and closed the door.

"You okay?" Max asked him.

"Yeah," he said but he looked pretty pale. "Seeing that didn't bother you?"

Max shrugged. "Looks like something from a video game. I guess he couldn't beat the Boss." Max shook his head. "It's nothing to laugh at, huh?"

But Sean laughed, in part because the stuff Max said was always kind of funny, but mostly because it was either laugh or puke and he sure didn't want to puke in front of all these people after he'd been on the force only three months. And he was not going back into that cabin, if he could avoid it.

"Did you see this?" Sean asked.

"Saw the whole thing," Max said.

"You'd better climb down and talk to Sergeant Grub."

"Grub? Like the worm? When did he come on?"

Sean laughed. "I wouldn't say that in front of him."

"One of those ... sensitive guys?"

Again Sean laughed. "Just go talk to him, Max."

"Gotcha." Max climbed down and walked toward the next cruiser as it pulled into the crowded lot, followed by yet another cruiser. I didn't know we had so many cruisers, he thought, and then, farther up the road he saw two more town cruisers and a state police cruiser behind them.

He walked over to Sgt. Grub, watching him climb out of his car, square his narrow shoulders, and hitch his gun belt up onto his stomach. The guy was short and plump and his skin was white as porcelain clay. "Sergeant, I'm Max Murphy. Sean said I should talk to you because I saw the whole thing."

"Not now," Sgt. Grub said, "can't you see I'm busy here? I've got an investigation to run. I've got to find out what happened."

Max grinned. "I'm a witness."

It made no impression. "Look, we'll get to you later, okay? First, we gotta find out what happened." He marched off like a politician, puffed up with his own self-importance.

Max walked to the back of the boat and stood off to the side, watching Grub walk around to the stern. He grabbed hold of the swim platform but he was too short and too plump and too weak to pull himself up. "Hey, Sean, give a hand here!"

Sean, who spent a lot of time lifting weights, reached down with one brawny arm, caught hold of the sergeant's wrist, and hauled him up onto the platform. "It's pretty nasty, Sergeant."

"How bad can it be?" He shook his head. "You rookies are all alike. You have to get used to this sort of thing in police work." He pushed past Sean, opened the door, then whirled around and rushed to the rail of the boat and began puking up his morning doughnuts, to a chorus of moans and groans from the crowd.

"Whoa," Max said to the woman standing next to him. "He hadn't even digested the rainbow sprinkles."

She looked around into his droll grin, ready to rip him a new lower outlet, or at least display how badly she'd been offended, and stopped. There was no way you could not grin back when Max Murphy grinned. It was as infectious as the flu. His black hair flopped down onto his forehead and his eyes were big and blue and they twinkled with irony. And when he smiled, big dimples broke out in his cheeks.

"Not the way to build confidence in our local police," Max said. "Now if he'd puked off the starboard side hardly anybody would have seen him. Not that we wouldn't have heard him, of course, but it would have been easier on the crowd."

"You have to be Max Murphy," the woman said.

"Yup."

"I thought so. I'm Tommy Simon's mother."

"Nice to meet you," Max said.

Chief Carl Murphy stepped onto the beach and walked toward the boat, spotting Max. He shook his head, took off his baseball cap, ran a hand over his thinning hair and replaced the cap. "I'm guessing you saw this, Max, is that right?" he asked.

"Sure did," Max said.

"How is it that every time something odd happens you're there?"

Max shrugged.

The Chief looked around, sniffing the air and wrinkling his nose. "What's that smell?"

"Grub evicted his morning doughnut ration," Max said.

Everyone standing nearby laughed nervously.

"Okay, Max, what's going on here?"

He stepped closer to his uncle. "The guy in the boat," he said very softly, "somebody cut his head off."

"What?"

"There's a machete covered with blood."

"No wonder Grub lost his breakfast."

"Probably not suicide," Max said. "Guy's got real short arms."

Carl chuckled. "Guess I better go take a look." He stepped to the stern just as Sgt. Grub decided to climb down, lost his footing, and with a great whoop, went flailing backward off the swim platform and into the water with a splash worthy of a giant squid. He lay, spread-eagled in the shallow water, his belly mounded upward like a dead fish bloated by the sun.

"Get me out! Get me out! I can't swim! I can't swim!"

Chief Murphy stood looking down at him in disbelief. "For God's sake, Grub, the water's only six inches deep!"

Grub was having none of it. "Help! Help!" he called. "I'm going down for the last time!" And because water generally gets deeper as you go out from the shore, Grub's head was just far enough out to go under, and he blew a spout worthy of a whale. His head came up and he gulped for air and down he went again.

Finally, Carl dropped off the swim platform, grabbed

Grub by the front of his shirt and pulled him onto his feet. "Get ahold of yourself, man! Get ahold of yourself. The water's only six inches deep!"

Grub looked down at the water which reached just above his ankles. "My head was under, Chief! I know my head was under!"

"Get a grip, man," Carl said as softly as he could. "Half the town is watching!"

Slowly, sheepishly Grub looked around. Then he reached down, grabbed his belt, and hiked up his pants. "I'm okay now," he said. "I'm okay. Thanks for saving me."

Carl shook his head. "Sergeant, go ask the trooper to put in a call to the state crime lab." He shook his head. "Then help the rest of the men organize the traffic. And get on the bull horn and ask for witnesses and take some statements."

"But Chief, I'm soaking wet."

"It's summer, Sergeant. You'll dry off."

"But what if my uniform shrinks, what'll ..."

"Sergeant!"

"Yes, Chief. Right away!"

Carl shook his head again, turned, and climbed easily up onto the boat where Sean was waiting. Max watched Sgt. Grub, curious now, wondering how anyone could behave like such a complete idiot. He was like the character in a movie who's only there to give the audience someone to laugh at.

"I offered to help him get down," Sean said.

"Never mind that. Let's have a look."

"It's pretty ugly, Chief." He stood back out of the way as Carl opened the door and stepped into the broad cabin.

He looked around carefully, not wanting to disturb anything until the crime lab got there, and then stepped back outside. "I've seen worse," he said, "but only in the war. Guess I'll have to agree with Max. Sure doesn't look like a suicide." He looked around. "In fact, at first blush, I'd say we're gonna have a murder to investigate." He took a deep breath. "You recognize him by any chance?"

Sean shook his head. "Don't even recognize the boat and the home port is Westbrook where I keep my boat."

Carl shrugged. "Oh well, no use to standing up here. I'll go see if there are any other witnesses besides Max, you see if you can't help Sgt. Grub with the traffic. We want to get as many people out of here as we can."

"Won't be easy, Chief. Kind of a strange sight."

"That it is. Post Henry up at the crossroad and tell him to divert the traffic. The rest of you tell everyone to leave, unless they saw what happened." He climbed over the gunwale and stood on the swim platform.

"Watch your footing there, Chief," Sean said.

Carl looked up and grinned. "Made it up, guess I can make it down." He jumped off the platform into the shallow water, then waded ashore and stopped when he came to Max.

He took out his notebook and a pen. "Can you tell me what happened? Exactly what happened?"

"Sure. Great big boat came up on the beach and ..." he pointed to the bits of ripped canvas and splintered wood sticking from beneath the hull of the boat ... "smashed my beach chair."

Carl shook his head and looked at his nephew. "No, Max. Tell me what really happened."

"Looks like a murder doesn't it," Max said.

Carl sighed. "Max, this is serious."

"It sure is," Max said, looking very somber. "That beach chair cost forty bucks. Mom is gonna be pretty unhappy."

"Max, you're trying my patience here."

"I told you what happened. I saw the boat coming, I hollered, and everyone got out of the way ..." He grinned and Carl looked at him warily. "But I won't lie to you, Uncle Carl, it was a close call with the porkers." He tipped his head toward the size 60s gathered like sows at a country fair.

TWO

Meeting Basil Greene

Word of the wreck had gotten around, of course, and at soccer practice that was all anyone wanted to hear about. Even Mr. Jenks, their coach, stood listening attentively as Max gave them a full and gory report. As he carefully offered up each nasty detail, Max kept his eye on a new blond-haired kid about his own height. There was nothing odd about somebody new turning up to try out because there were always the summer kids and then too, new people kept moving in all the time, but there was something about the guy, an air of confidence maybe, or an attitude. Probably the latter. Lots of the summer kids came with attitudes. It went with the turf. Money, big houses, private schools, and fancy cars always produced an attitude. And yet … that didn't seem to hit the mark.

"Wow!" Charlie Gray said, "his head was actually cut off?"

Max nodded, his black hair flopping. "His head was on one side of the cabin and his body was on the other, and there was a bloody machete in the middle."

"Way gross ..." Tom Pringle said. He looked kind of gray, almost as if he were ready to blow his lunch.

"Then the cops got there and the new guy, Sergeant Grub, took one look and tossed his cookies, doughnuts, actually, over the side of the boat."

"Gross, way, way gross," Tom Pringle said again, his face pinching up as if he were about to follow in Grub's footsteps.

"What did the police say?" Mr. Jenks asked.

"Not much. The guys from the crime lab had just gotten there when I left. They were stretching yellow tapes everywhere and people were already starting to complain about not being able to use the beach."

"Well, I can certainly understand that," Coach Jenks said. "It's a town beach, you know."

Max laughed. "Sure, and with weather like this everybody wants to be on the beach."

"It's their right as taxpayers," the coach said.

"How come the boat didn't tip over onto its side?" Wally Hinkman asked.

"It was going so fast that the bow cut a huge groove in the sand when the boat ran up onto the beach," Max said.

"Who was it?" Sam Fine asked. "Anybody we know?"

"I couldn't see the face," Max said.

"Okay, guys," Mr. Jenks said, "time to get started. We've got just four days before our first game against Clinton and from what I hear they've got a whole bunch of summer kids who are aces." He looked over at the new guy standing on the edge of the group. "But we've got one too." He pointed. "Meet Basil Greene. He was all-prep New England at striker as a sophomore last fall and he lives here full time when he's not in school. He comes from England."

Basil got the usual once over, the furtive, grudging glances that carried a clear message about territory and having to prove your reputation. And then Max made the connection. The new family that had moved into the old Gottlieb place. Hadn't he heard that the guy was an English lord? Something like that, he was sure of it.

"Max is our only goalie. I had hoped that Preston would be available but he's working full time this summer, so Max is the man in goal."

"Yeah, go Mad Max," Charlie said.

Max grinned. If Preston were here he'd be starting in goal. Jenks played his favorites and only let the younger guys play when the others had graduated. It explained why his teams never went anywhere, which was why it sucked playing soccer for the high school. But that was something he'd have to live with. Mad Max Murphy didn't much like the idea. In fact, he hated it, but he couldn't change it either.

At least now he had a chance to show what he could do. And once they had warmed up and begun shooting drills the spotlight was on him. He stopped shot after shot, tipping them away with either his feet or his hands, smothering them when they came straight at him, leaping to deflect the high shots. He was like a wild man, and nothing got past him.

Then they switched drills, going to passes that led the shooter inside the big rectangle around the goal; the box, sacred ground. You never allowed a shot from inside the box. Give 'em a corner kick, anything but a straight-on shot from inside the box.

In this drill, with no defensemen to harass the shooter, most goalies only stopped the bad shots. It was an anti-goalie drill, designed more for the shooters than for the goalie, and Max decided to turn it around. This was his territory, his turf and he challenged every invader, coming out hard to cut down their angles, waving his arms, diving into their cleats, anything to disrupt their timing.

It worked perfectly until Basil came in, took the pass with his right foot, and from two steps inside the box let go a powerful drive that blew past Max's fingertips and into the net. Max picked himself up from the ground, retrieved the ball and called out. "Hey, Greene, great shot, man!"

No one else said anything but they saw it, and now they knew why he was all-prep. The guy had a cannon. Even so, Max thought, I should have got to it, but I could've sworn he was going left and instead he went right and I didn't pick up on it. Okay, next time, I stop him. And when Basil started his next turn, Max discovered he wasn't ready for Basil Greene, who took the pass, pivoted as if he were going for the same corner and instead came through with his left foot and caught Max flatfooted. This guy is good, Max thought, he is really good. He must have played a lot of soccer in England.

But the third time it didn't work. It was a good move but Max had pushed himself into yet another gear and when Basil picked up the pass and started through with his right foot, Max dove to his left, sure that's where the ball had to go. But Basil kicked past the ball with his right foot, pivoted and started through with his left foot, just pooching the ball to the right. Max rolled into a somersault, then using the goal post for leverage, threw himself into a back flip and then stretched as far as he could and deflected the shot with his right hand.

"Way to go," Basil called. "That was a truly great stop!"

"If you'd hit it a little harder, I'd never have got to it."

"Even so, I never saw a better stop … ever."

"To cook a pancake, you gotta flip 'em," Max said.

After practice, Max stripped off his sweaty shirt and pulled a dry tee shirt from his gear bag. He might have felt better about himself in the past, he thought, but it would be hard to say when because this day had been a ten.

"Max, can I talk to you for a minute?" Coach Jenks said.

It wasn't a question you answered and worse, he could tell from the tone of voice the coach used, the superior, slightly troubled sound that adults always used when they were going to say something they thought was for your benefit, that this was not going to make him happy.

"You looked pretty good out there today, Max. And you certainly stopped a lot of shots. But when you play for me you have to learn to be less flamboyant. Like that play when you turned the back flip. I just can't have that sort of stuff on one of my teams."

"Right," Max said. "Front flips only from now on."

"That, ahh, that really wasn't what I meant, Max. What I mean is no flips."

Max looked at him carefully to find out whether he was being put on. He wasn't. "It wasn't for show," he said, "it was the only way I could get back for the shot."

"Well, I'm sure you could have got it some other way. You see, it's important for the team that nobody stand out like that. It embarrasses the other players."

"Right, Coach," he said, "avoiding embarrassment is the main thing. I understand that clearly now and I'll be sure to avoid it in the future. And I'll also be sure not to embarrass the other teams too because while we want to win, we don't want our victories to be at anyone else's expense."

Coach Jenks smiled. "I'm glad to hear you say that, Max. It shows you're part of the team."

Somewhere behind him and not too far away he heard Basil laugh and in those few seconds a mutual admiration society formed between Mad Max Murphy and Basil Greene. Had anyone predicted such an alliance they'd have been hooted out of town. Here was Mad Max Murphy whose family had been here for over two hundred years; whose parents ran a bar and restaurant called The Crab Trap, known both for particularly good food and wild times.

On the weekends the place was so packed and the music so loud it threatened to blow the roof off the building. Take a crowd that size, soak them in alcohol, and people begin to disagree, which was why Tom Murphy had two bouncers and an off-duty cop on hand to cap off any disturbance.

And because the restaurant was located on the river that divided Guilford and Madison, the common solution for overheated humans was to toss them into a cooler solution ... the river. It worked uncommonly well. And when the tide was right, the diners in the restaurant at the back of the building, which looked out over the marsh, were treated to the sight of drifting revellers fighting their way to shore. Tom also employed a lifeguard on the off chance that someone got too drunk to fight the current or had never learned to swim. And whenever a new guy showed up, the regulars taunted him and badgered him until he blew his cool and qualified for a "cooling off". It didn't always work, but there were plenty of hotheads around and sooner or later somebody went for a swim.

On weekdays, after four, the bar drew in the working men; electricians, plumbers, carpenters, builders, wood cutters, garbage collectors, skunk removers, excavators, and fishermen, and the word was that no matter what you wanted to get done, after four o'clock you could find someone to do it at The Trap.

There were complaints, as you might expect, from the "better" families in town, meaning those who had moved in recently; those who thought they occupied some elevated social position because they'd paid a million bucks for their house or well over a million if they lived on the water, but when your brother is the chief of police and the family has their fingers in nearly every pie in town, such sniveling is easily shrugged off. After all, the whiners were all new people who had "discovered" the town and felt that the shenanigans at The Crab Trap should not be allowed. Slowly, such folk discovered that the louder they complained, the longer it took to get their septic tanks pumped, or their driveways plowed, or anything on the house fixed.

Basil, on the other hand, had spent a good number of his years in English private schools, which they call public schools (but then they also drive on the wrong side of the road), particularly at Eton. His father, an archaeologist of world renown, had been offered a professorship at Yale, an endowed chair which, though it came with a high salary, would not have supported the lifestyle they were accustomed to in England. But Basil Greene III, Lord Harrowfield, actually, was a very wealthy man from an extraordinarily wealthy family, so the salary had played no role in his decision to take the job at Yale. Instead it was the chance to work with two other famous archaeologists in the department there.

They did not live in the style they had enjoyed at home. They had no servants, they drove sedate looking Lincolns, and they did not keep horses for riding to the hounds. They had bought a house on the water, a rather large house, to be sure, but there were plenty of such houses in Madison.

None of that mattered to either Max or Basil. They were both athletes and they recognized in each other a different sort of elitism, one based on ability and nothing else. Well, there was one other thing. Max drew other kids to him the way flowers draw bees. The same charm, however was lost on adults who usually assumed his wry grin was nothing more than arrogance. What they did not understand was the difference between someone who is cocky and someone who is cocksure. Max was not conceited, he was confident. So too, was Basil. And like Max he drew his confidence from his ability on the field, though he was also a brilliant student whereas Max regarded classes as something he had to pass in order to play soccer.

Such friendships are never spoken. They just occur.

Three

The Chicken In The Road

They sat on the grass in the shade of a big sugar maple behind the old school in the center of town, waiting for their rides.

"Max," Basil said, "how did you learn to do that?"

"Do what?"

"To start off being reprimanded by the coach and in the end getting him to agree not to win any games."

"It only works with someone who isn't listening. You tell him what he expects to hear, only you don't."

"I also saw that move you put on Hinkman."

"It took him by surprise. It's what life is all about; taking people by surprise."

Basil looked at him. "Where do you learn this stuff?"

"I make it up as I go. But I gotta tell you, it's gotten me into a boat load of trouble."

"I shouldn't wonder." He grinned. "Still, it must be God's own amount of fun." He ran a hand over his sweaty hair, flattening it against his head. "Now, tell me more about the headless yachtsman."

Max's deep blue eyes twinkled with irony. "He crushed my beach chair."

Basil smiled and shook his head. "That's it?"

"Absolutely crunched it. Lucky I wasn't asleep." He looked out at the street, feeling Basil looking at him, waiting for more. He shrugged. "There was one thing that was odd, other than the fact that the owners of forty-foot boats don't normally try to park them in the lot at West Wharf. There was something about it that stuck in my mind but I can't quite put my finger on it."

"Déjà vu, eh what?"

"Yeah."

"Does this sort of thing happen to you often?"

"So far only when a big yacht runs up onto the beach and crushes my beach chair. It was an expensive chair."

Basil chuckled. "No, I mean, are you always around when strange things occur?"

"All the time. Like last week. I was sitting out in front of the restaurant eating my lunch when a car pulled in. There must have been ten people inside this little Honda Civic and they were screaming and thrashing around and when the car stopped they all jumped out and began running in circles, slapping at themselves, and the car just kept on going, right over the seawall, and plunged into the creek." He laughed. "It was awesome!"

"Did you ever find out how it happened?"

"Sure. A yellow jacket flew in through the window and the driver went crazy." He shook his head. "Man, you should've heard the hollering and screaming. And then, when their car plunged into the creek, it sounded as if Ghengis Khan had dropped by to commit a little friendly carnage."

Basil looked closely at his new acquaintance. "Where did you learn to talk like that?"

"My mother watched a lot of Robin Williams movies when she was pregnant."

"Okay," Basil said, "I have a question."

"Shoot."

"When will they know what happened on the yacht?"

"I'll be talking to Uncle Carl later."

"Who's Uncle Carl?"

"The police chief."

"Now that's what I call well-connected."

Max grinned. "It's good for business."

"Oh?"

"Dad owns The Crab Trap."

"Really? That's a very good restaurant. We ate there just the other night. My father says it's the best food he's eaten at a restaurant since we came over. Adored the place. Even likes the bar. He and Mum go there for drinks at least once a week. Says it's totally American."

"I heard your father has a title, is that true?"

Basil looked suddenly wary, his eyes narrowing. "We try not to make much of that over here."

"What kind of title?"

"Well, actually, he's the tenth Earl of Harrowfield."

"What's he called?"

"Lord Greene."

"An actual English lord … now that's impressive."

"Not really, well, I mean, there aren't an awful lot of earls, but it's just something he inherited, you see."

"And will you be the eleventh Earl of Harrowfield?"

Basil grinned. "Can you live with that?"

"You could be the next pope for all I care, as long as you don't let it get in the way of your game." He raised one eyebrow as he looked around at Basil. "But no bowing. It's bad for the stomach and probably violates the Constitution."

"Right. No bowing. Odious business. No 'M'lords' or 'M'ladys' either. I've always hated that sort of thing, but there's not much one can do about it. And one day I'll be Lord Harrowfield and I'll probably even like it."

"Pretty classy."

"Or maybe I'll just stay here. Then I won't have to follow in my father's footsteps."

"Nobody much does that here. Not that it doesn't happen. My brother Wayne is going to culinary school because he loves to cook and he's going to step right into the business. But I'm not working in a restaurant. In the first place it's all night work. I don't even like to eat in restaurants."

"What then?"

"I think first I'll go to college and then I'll start trying to figure it out."

"And that way you get to play football, oops, sorry, soccer, for another four years."

"That did occur to me."

"Where'd you learn to play goal that way?"

Max shrugged. "It's just the way I play, I guess. I mean it's not like I ever saw anyone who played that way. I just kind of do what I need to."

"Well, it is nothing short of awesome."

"Thanks. Maybe I'll do okay if I don't run into any guys who've got a bag of tricks like yours."

"The difficulty with things like that is you never get to use them in a game unless you get a clean break past the defense. You know how often that happens? Maybe once a season. Most shots are just a reaction to what happens on the field."

"Hey, I got an idea. Do you water ski?"

"Yes, actually, done quite a bit of it on the Riviera."

"Whoa ... the French place on the Italian ocean." He slapped his hands against his knees. "Well, okay then. I've got a fast boat and all we need is someone to watch for us."

"My sister will go. She's a great skier too, both water and snow. You should have seen her last year at Vengen. Magnificent. Put us all to shame."

"Take me about an hour after I get home."

"Sounds like fun."

"Sometimes the water's pretty choppy but there's not much wind today."

"How big is your boat?"

"Twenty-four feet. It's got two one hundred and thirty horse Hondas. It'll do over forty knots."

"Fast enough, I should think."

"Yours is the cottage on the point past East Wharf?"

Basil nodded.

As always, Max was not shy about asking questions. "What's it like at Choate?"

"Vastly different from school at home, but I like it quite well, actually."

"What's your coach like?"

"A bit of the old sod. Played professionally in England before he blew out a knee. Tough. You do it his way or you're gone. Has his degree from Oxford, worked for some branch of the bloody government but he won't say which. All very hush-hush, top secret, that sort of thing. Something like your CIA, I should think." He looked around at Max.

"You'd like him. He only plays the lads with talent."

"Sounds like my kind of a guy." He pointed to a black Lincoln turning the corner. "This your ride?"

Basil stood. "About an hour?"

"Maybe longer. I may have to get gas for the boat."

"I'll be watching for you."

Max watched the car disappear up the street and wondered where his mother had gotten to. Probably working. He looked down at his watch. Pretty late for the lunch crowd, but in the summer all bets were off. Sometimes the lunch people were just leaving when people began to show up for dinner.

He looked up as Mrs. Santorini wobbled down her front walk, leaning on her cane, but still making pretty good time. She was short and very round, and since her husband had died she dressed only in black. She even wore a black saucer-shaped hat covered with long black trailing feathers. It didn't take much imagination to conjure up a big chicken, Max thought.

She stopped at the curb, looked to her right, then stepped into the street, never seeing the bright red BMW coming from her left. It was too late to shout or to run or to do anything but watch and, fortunately, the driver had also been watching and he slammed on his brakes and stopped within two feet of Mrs. Santorini.

The driver, a tall, broad-shouldered man with dark hair, leaped out of his car and walked up to her, clearly concerned, starting to apologize, but before he got a single word out, Mrs. Santorini up and whacked him right on the old coconut with her cane. "Run an old woman down will you!" she shouted in her crackly voice. She hit him again on his well-muscled arms as he raised them to protect his head, and then, before he could adjust, she snapped the cane from the side and nailed him in the shins. Now the guy was dancing as if he were hopping barefoot over hot coals.

"Ow! Stop that! You're hurting me! What's the matter with you? Are you crazy?"

She changed tactics and began poking him in the chest with the knobby black stick. "The trouble with this world is that no one respects their elders!" she shouted at him. "Running down old people in broad daylight! Ought to have you drawn and quartered!" She drew the cane up again but the guy darted for his car, climbed in, and wound up the windows.

Mrs. Santorini was not deterred. She simply crashed the cane down onto the hood of the car.

The driver threw it into reverse and squealed his tires as he tore back out of range.

"Aha!" she shouted. "Disturbing the peace!"

The car sat quietly in the sun as Mrs. Santorini weighed her options. At close range she could wield her cane like an Olympic fencer. But now he was out of range and her sprinting days were long past.

"Coward!" She waved her cane at him. "Come back and take your whipping like a man! Or are you just another one of those yellow-bellied suburbanites?"

The car didn't move and things had clearly reached a stalemate. Mrs. Santorini squared her shoulders, finished crossing the street, walked to the end, and then recrossed the street as she headed for the village, which left Max to puzzle over why she had bothered to cross the street in the first place.

The car rolled slowly forward and when it stopped across

from where Max was sitting, the driver got out and inspected the damage to his hood. He shook his head and turned toward Max. "Did you see that? he asked. "That woman is crazy!" He wiped his forehead with the back of his hand. "Who is she?"

"Mrs. Santorini."

"Did you see her hit my car? I mean, bad enough she hit me, but why did she hit my car?"

"'Cause you were inside it," Max said.

"But this is a brand new BMW!"

"She never plays favorites."

The man shook his head. "People like that should be locked up."

"You must be new in town," Max said, knowing he had never seen the guy before, and wondering how he had kept from grabbing the cane. He looked like the kind of guy you didn't mess with and yet he had shown not the least sign of aggression toward Mrs. Santorini.

"What's that got to do with anything?"

"People who've been here awhile have learned to watch out for her."

"Me? I have to look out? What did I do? She never looked before stepping into the street!"

"She only looks to the right. She says trouble always comes from the right. Her husband was a union mason."

The man blinked as if trying to compute what Max had said. "You can't just go around hitting people. It's against the law! I'm going to report this to the police."

Max shook his head. "Won't work," he said. "The chief is her son in law."

"You know I was just about to buy a house in this town, but now I'm having second thoughts."

"That's just as well," Max said. "There's too many Beemers already. You'd probably have to get yourself a Jaguar or something." Max grinned and the strange, detached quality of that grin seemed to confuse the driver even more.

"Too many Beemers? The town has too many Beemers?"

"And just this morning a guy got his head cut off."

"What?"

"On a boat. His head was on one side of the ..."

"That's it! That's enough. I'm out of here!" He jumped into his car, stomped on the gas and roared off down the street and around the corner, the tires howling as he headed for Route 79. Bad idea, Max thought. Sean's probably sitting in the parking lot waiting for people to run the light. He grinned as he heard the siren go off. That was one less Beemer owner in town. James Madison would have been proud of him. Or would he? Was the town even named for him? How come nobody in school ever mentioned that? All he ever heard about was Prudence Crandall and George Washington Carver. What about old George Washington himself?

His mother pulled the old blue GMC pickup in close to the curb and Max opened the door and climbed in.

"Anything exciting happen?"

"Mrs. Santorini caned some guy in a Beemer."

"Tried to run her down, right?"

"Same old, same old. She won't look to her left. But I think she does it on purpose. She crossed the street, walked to the corner, and crossed back over. Maybe she really is crazy."

They started for home. "Carl says she's trying to work up a lawsuit."

"What if somebody hits her?"

"Then she gets her day in court."

"Not if she's dead."

"Anna? Not a chance."

"But I mean, she walks with a cane. How could she get out of the way?"

"The cane's just for show."

"It's for more than that. She could have fought with William Wallace." He shook his head as he thought about trying to dodge out of the way of an oncoming car. "No way is she quick enough. If she keeps it up she's gonna get whacked, Mom."

"She may get whacked, but she won't get any money out of it. Carl will testify that she did it on purpose."

"Whoa, no more hot meals for that dude."

She laughed. "You got that right."

"Probably have to farm out his laundry too." He looked around at his mother. "I'm gonna take the boat over to Basil's, is that okay?"

"Who's Basil?"

"New kid in town. Basil Greene."

"Sounds like something you put in a salad."

Max grinned. There was no doubt about where his odd sense of humor had come from. And then another image crept in as he thought of Mrs. Santorini. A big, black chicken. But at least in this case, he knew why the chicken crossed the road.

Four

The Floater

Even though they lived well out toward the end of Mungertown Road, it took less than a half hour to reach Harbor Avenue on his Cannondale racer. He left it at one of the cottages they rented out each summer and walked down to the crowded beach, carrying a pair of oars, the water skis, and the towrope.

You knew it was summer, he thought, when you walked one of the roads to the beach and the smell of the tall privet hedges blended with the thick salty air. Why couldn't he remember what it smelled like in the fall or the winter? He made a note to think about that.

Halfway down the road to the beach, Sgt. Grub pulled up alongside him and stopped. "Hey," he called out his window, "where you going with all that stuff?"

Max stopped and looked into the cruiser. "Who? Me?"

"Yeah you." He climbed out of the cruiser and walked around the front of the car, hitching his gun belt up onto his stomach. "I don't want any trouble out of you."

Max eased the skis from his shoulder and leaned them against the hedge.

"We've had a string of break-ins around here."

"Yeah, I heard that."

"So where did you get all that stuff?"

"From my garage," Max said. He decided to leave Uncle Carl out of this.

"And where do you think you're going with it?"

"Down to my boat."

"Right. You own a boat."

"My dad owns the boat."

"And you have a license for that boat."

"As a matter of fact I do. It's on the boat."

Grub hooked his thumbs under his gunbelt, then pushed his hat back on his head and pulled out his notebook. "Okay, where are you going with that boat?"

"Water skiing." He pointed to the skis. "That's why I was carrying water skis."

"And where are you going to be water skiing?"

Max shook his head. Something was seriously out of whack here. "That's my business," he said.

"When a police officer asks you a question, you answer."

The voice had changed. Suddenly it sounded hard and it dripped with authority, and Max decided he was through with Sgt. Grub. He picked up the skis, set them on his shoulder and turned toward the water at the end of the street.

"Where do you think you're going?"

Max grinned. "Water skiing."

"Not until I say so," Grub said.

Max stopped and turned. "Look Sergeant, I haven't done anything wrong here and I know enough about the law to know that I don't have to answer any of your questions. I don't want any trouble, I just want to get to my boat so I can go skiing."

"You going alone?"

Max laughed. He didn't think he'd ever heard a dumber question. "Absolutely," he said. "I just put the boat on auto-pilot and run a cable down the tow rope so I can control the boat from there."

"You're pushing me pretty hard here, kid," Grub said. "I know what my rights are."

"Maybe I oughta take you in."

"Bad idea," Max said. "Take my word for it."

"You got a smart mouth, you know that?"

"Nothing new there."

"Okay, that's it, you're under arrest!"

"For what?"

"Disrespect."

"Maybe you better ask my name first."

"You think that'll change things?"

"Maybe not, but you're gonna need it when we get to the station, anyway."

"Okay, give me a name."

"Maxwell Murphy"

"Where'd you get a name like that?"

"The phone book."

"You must think I'm pretty dumb, huh?"

"The name doesn't sound familiar?"

"Never heard it before."

"How about the last part?"

"Murphy? Lots of people named Murphy."

"Especially when it's the same as the chief of police."

"You're saying you're related to the Chief. You gotta do better than that, kid."

"The chief is my uncle, and I gotta tell you Sergeant, you're not much of a cop. You should've asked me that first and then gotten an address."

"How do I know you're not lying?"

Max dropped the tow rope, unslung his knapsack, and started to put his hand inside.

"Hold it! Hold it right there!" Grub put his hand on the Glock in his holster.

Max opened the bag, bent over and dumped the contents on the ground. Then he picked up the cell phone and dialed up the police station.

"Mrs. Field, it's Max. Is Uncle Carl there?"

"He's busy, Max."

"Mrs. Field, could you tell him that Sergeant Grub is here trying to arrest me for carrying gear down to the boat and I don't think he really wants to do that."

"Hold on."

"Max?"

"Hi, Uncle Carl. Sorry to bother you, but I've got a little problem here."

"Put him on, Max."

He handed the phone to Grub.

"Hello?" Grub said. "Yes, Chief. I caught him red-handed. Well, he was carrying stuff."

Even from where he was standing he could hear Uncle Carl shout; "get your fat butt in that car and get back here!"

"Okay, Chief." He handed the phone to Max, scowling. "Something important came up. I've got to get back to the station." He pointed at Max. "But I'll be watching you, and closely from now on!"

Max shrugged, turned, and walked toward the beach. The guy was a total nutbag. How'd he ever get to be a cop, let alone a sergeant? Uncle Carl must be losing it, he thought.

There were several girls his age on the beach and a couple of guys, but he didn't recognize any of them, nor would he likely get to know them unless they were there for the summer, or at the least for a month. It was just the way it worked in a shore town or, he supposed, in any town, but he couldn't be certain about that because he had only ever lived in Madison.

He flipped the dinghy, put the gear in, put on his life jacket, and dragged the boat over the sand and down to the water. The Sound was calm, with only soft waves a few inches high as he pushed the eight foot boat into the water, climbed in, dropped the oars into the oarlocks, and began rowing out past the basking kids on the swimming raft to where the boat swung on its mooring.

The bright colors of the beach umbrellas and people in brilliant bathing suits marked the contrast between summer and the rest of the year. Come September, the cottages would be closed up except for occasional weekends, the boats would mostly have been hauled, and the town would settle back to normal, though not the way it once had, at least according to his folks.

Then there had been only five thousand winter residents instead of around fifteen thousand and they had rolled up the streets at night. Now the center of town hummed like a beehive year-round. Max didn't think he'd have liked the old way much. Just not enough going on, though, in fact, not a whole lot went on even now unless you could drive. And by September he'd have his license. Man, would that be cool.

The dinghy bumped up against the twenty-four foot

Mako and he clipped the bow line to the eye bolt on the stern, set the water skis and the tow rope into the boat, and climbed aboard. The only cover was on the console in the center of the boat and he pulled it free, folded it and stowed it in the compartment on the right side.

He put the key into the ignition and turned on the power. The big outboards started on the first try and he let them idle as he picked up the boat hook, unclipped the dinghy and led it forward. Using the pole he hauled the boat up toward the mooring buoy tied to the hundred pound mushroom anchor on the bottom. He clipped the dinghy to the ring in the line, unclipped the mooring line, and then walked back aft.

When the bow drifted away from the mooring, he dropped the engines into gear and idled out past the mooring and then the rocks until he reached deep water. Then he cranked it up. The two big engines slammed the boat forward driving the hull up onto the surface of the water in a plane as he put the helm over and headed east toward Basil's, the boat making a good forty knots. It was a perfect day for skiing, the water flat but for the low swells that never disappeared altogether, and the boat just ate those up as if they weren't there.

Out on the Sound it looked like a boat owner's convention, with all sorts of sailboats and powerboats headed in every possible direction. It was one of the things he liked best about being on the water. No roads. You could go any way you chose and all you had to watch for were rocks and sandbars. But he knew them all by heart from here east to Old Saybrook and to Branford on the west.

He knew them because he had been forced to memorize them from the charts. Not fun. Not any fun at all, but until he had them down, his father wouldn't let him take the boat out alone. The safe-boating course had been a joke compared to having had to learn the charts. The real brain bender had been the Power Squadron course. And though he would never admit it to his father, it had been the right thing to do. He looked shoreward as he came up on the Surf Club. The place was crawling with people.

He flew on past, adjusting his course to take him outside Tuxis Island so he wouldn't have to reduce speed to five miles an hour in the mooring, and then he changed his mind and aimed at the inside passage. This way he got to show off the boat and the fact that he was the pilot. A little profiling never hurt, after all.

As he chugged through the passage, he realized that he was backtracking the path the yacht had taken that morning,

He glanced back over his shoulder and the yacht was still there, only now there was a huge tugboat and a barge with a crane moored in behind the stone jetty. It was almost as if it hadn't happened. Strange how something so nasty could fade so quickly. The images he carried in his head could just as easily have come from a movie.

Once past the moorings he opened up the engines and blasted by East Wharf then made a wide sweeping turn in toward Basil's. He saw him stand up and wave and then a girl also stood up and even from a hundred yards off he could tell this was no ordinary girl.

Basil directed him around the point to a small pier and Max brought the boat in slowly and then, as he approached the pier, put the engines into reverse and brought the boat up softly against the bumpers. It was a slick little piece of seamanship and it did not go unnoticed.

"Nicely done," Basil said. He took the line Max tossed him and warped it over a cleat on the pier. "This is my little sister Margaret, Meg for short."

Max smiled. She was a very good-looking girl. Her face was narrow and she had high cheekbones and blond hair the color of pale honey and huge blue eyes and a wonderful tan. She smiled back.

"Not so little, Basil," he said, and he knew he'd said just the right thing when Meg's smile grew even wider.

"I'm only a year younger, but to hear Basil, you'd think I still wore nappies."

Max laughed.

"You know what nappies are?" Basil asked.

"I read Dick Francis novels," Max said.

"Bravo!" Meg said. "Isn't he just super?"

"She's a little balmy when it comes to horses," Basil said.

"Not much on horses," Max said, "but I like his books." He swung his hand toward the boat. "Climb aboard and let's get going."

Meg, tall and slender, stepped easily into the boat , moving with the grace and ease of a cheetah. Max shook his head. Girls. One look and they turned him inside out, especially girls that looked like Meg Greene. And the blue bikini she wore only made it worse. It was gonna be a long afternoon, he thought, as Basil came aboard with the line and Max backed the boat out and turned the bow toward the open water.

"Okay," he said, "here's the rules. We always have somebody watching the skier and everybody wears a life vest."

"I hate life vests," Meg said.

"Right. Messes up the tan," Basil said.

"They're too hot," Meg said.

Max shifted to neutral and while the boat was drifting, he stepped to the stern, opened the hatch and pulled out a five gallon bucket. He dipped it over the side and set the half-full pail on the deck.

"What's that for?" Basil asked.

"Hot people," Max said as he dropped back onto the seat behind the wheel. He looked around at them and grinned. "With a bikini like that you may need to douse me about every ten minutes."

Basil laughed and Meg blushed.

"I told you," Basil said to his sister. "He says the most extraordinary things."

Meg was still blushing as she clipped on the life vest and zipped it closed. He was also, she thought, much better looking than Basil had told her, and while he wasn't as broadly built as her brother, he was very well built and he looked strong and very athletic. But the best thing was his grin and the way his eyes bored right into you, completely focused. It was extremely flattering. Things were definitely picking up in the boy department, she thought.

"Okay, who's first?" Max asked as he clipped the end of the towrope to the stern, then slipped on the floating handle and paid the line out carefully into the water to make sure it didn't tangle.

"I'll go," Meg said.

Max stepped back to the wheel, checking to make sure the engines were in neutral. He knew they were, but you always checked, especially when anyone was in the water near the boat.

"Okay, Meg, jump in and we'll get going."

Meg slipped over the side, and put on the skis as Basil handed them to her and then she picked up the tow rope handle.

Max put the engines in gear and slowly pulled out until the line drew taut.

"Ready," he said to Basil.

"Ready, Meg?" Basil called.

"Ready!"

Max slammed the throttles forward and the surge of the boat pulled Meg cleanly up onto the surface. She took a second to adjust her trim and get her balance and then she began cutting back and forth across the wake, jumping from the top each time and then she began pivoting, doing three-sixties. The longer she skied, the more her confidence grew and pretty soon she was leaping high off the wake and turning three-sixties in the air.

The whole time Basil sat with his eyes riveted on his sister. Max ran the boat, occasionally turning back to catch a glimpse of Meg high in the air. The temptation just to turn and watch her pulled at him as if he'd been haltered and someone kept jerking the lead rope. But he resisted the pressure, only allowing himself an occasional glance and then only when the way ahead was absolutely clear for a long, long way.

They were nearly to Meig's Point when Basil tapped him on the shoulder. "She wants a rest."

Max pulled back on the throttle and the boat dropped down into the water. He shifted into reverse and Basil began taking in the line, coiling it neatly. Well before they reached Meg, Max shifted to neutral and let her swim the rest of the way to the boat. He got ready to help her aboard, but she reached up with both hands, grabbed the gunwale and using a dolphin kick, snapped herself upward and onto the boat.

"That was great, Max! This is a very fast boat."

He grinned. "Pretty neat work out there," he said. "Looks like you've spent some time on the end of a rope."

They spent another two hours skiing and Max took his turn but he resisted the urge to show off. He didn't do a single flip, his best trick, and the most he allowed himself were several extremely high leaps.

They sat in the boat, towels draped over their shoulders, as Max carefully coiled the line and stowed the gear in the stern compartment.

"How'd you like something to drink?" Basil asked.

"Sure," Max said.

"We can tie up at the pier."

"Okay."

"And we'll chip in on the petrol," Meg said.

"No, this time is my treat," Max said.

"Next time?" Meg asked.

"Sure." It was hard to even look at her and not go all wobble-legged.

Max dropped the engines into forward, turned the wheel, and they headed home, cruising along at about thirty knots. Just past Hammonasset, before the cottages started, Max spotted something drifting closer in toward shore and he swung the bow toward it. Later, when he thought about it, he could not think what had prompted him to do that because there was nothing unusual about stuff floating in the Sound.

As they came nearer he slowed the boat to idle and both Basil and Meg stood up to look. Before they got close enough to see what it was, Max knew and he turned the boat away.

"What is it, Max?" Basil asked.

He looked at them. "How strong is your stomach?"
They both looked mystified.
"Maybe it would be better if you didn't look."
"A body!" Meg did not look happy.
"Two in one day, old boy!" Basil laughed.
"Pretty weird. Must be a sign. Probably means I should become an undertaker."
"Doesn't it bother you?" Meg asked.
"It's dead," Max said. He reached into his gear bag, took out the cell phone, and punched in a number. "Uncle Carl needs to know about this, and I need to know what to do." He waited and then spoke. "Hi, Mrs. Field, this is Max Murphy, can you get Uncle Carl for me?"
"He's busy, Max."
He frowned. "Yes, but this is an emergency."
"Perhaps you'd better tell me what this is all about."
"Well, I'd rather tell him, if it's all the same." He waited, rolling his eyes upward and shaking his head.
"This line is for police business, Max."
"Mrs. Field, this is police business! Do you think I'd call if it weren't? I know that he's busy, I mean, he doesn't have a murder on his hands every day, but I really need to talk to him, okay?"
He looked around at Basil and Meg. "They don't trust kids," he said. "They think we're all a bunch of doped up potheads." He looked back toward the body bobbing slowly in the gentle swells. "Hi, Uncle Carl, listen, I'm out here just past Hammonasset in the boat, about a half-mile off-shore and there's a body floating."
"Another one?"
"It's a woman this time. Do you want me to tow it in?"
"No, Max, I'll come out. Can you mark it?"

He nodded. "In fact, I'd rather do that. I can give you the coordinates from the GPS too."

"Good, do that."

"Be a second."

Max turned on the GPS, located his position and wrote it down. Then he dictated it to Uncle Carl. "It'll drift some on the tide, but you should be able to spot the marker. I've got an old lobster pot buoy."

"Good. We shouldn't have any trouble. Call me later. We'll need to talk."

"Sure." He grinned. "And tell Mrs. Field that Mad Max is not happy over having been given the third degree." He laughed. "Yeah, okay, see you later." He switched off the phone.

"Are we really going to drag it in?" Meg looked pale beneath her tan.

Max opened one of the compartments along the side of the boat. "No. I'm going to attach a buoy."

"How are you going to attach it?" Basil asked, sounding more than a little anxious.

"With this." Max held up a large bluefish jig. He pulled out a spool of monofilament fish line, tied the end to the hook then reeled off several feet before cutting the line and tying it to an orange lobster pot buoy. "I'll pull alongside, hook the jig into the clothing and then we can go. I don't know how strong your stomachs are, but if this is anything like the one this morning, maybe you'd better not look."

"Do things like this happen to you often?" Basil asked.

"Not bodies. Bodies are new. But other weird stuff … I don't know, I just happen to be around, I guess."

Max shifted to forward and worked his way slowly back

to the body, shifting to neutral as he came close and then tossing the jig onto the back and jerking the line to set the hook. Then he tossed the buoy overboard and quickly stepped to the helm.

"Hang on," he said as he pushed the throttles forward and the boat leaped up into a plane.

As he brought the boat in toward shore, he saw the Harbor Patrol boat come past East Wharf at full speed. At the pier, Basil jumped out and tied up the boat as Max shut down the engines.

"Tell me something," Meg said. "Did that body seem to be missing something?"

Max nodded. "Its head."

"Just like the one this morning, is that right?" Basil asked.

"How terrible," Meg said.

Max grinned. "Probably won't be doing an open casket for this one either."

Both Basil and Meg laughed, uneasily at first, and finally with greater enthusiasm as they discovered how laughing helped tame the horror of what they had seen.

Five

Discoveries

They sat on the wide veranda drinking Pepsis and looking out across the Sound.

"Do you think she was murdered?" Meg asked.

"People seldom cut their own heads off," Basil said. "You'd need a motorized guillotine."

"God, I don't believe I said that. Talk about a stupid question! You'd think I was competing for blond-of-the-month!"

Max and Basil both laughed with her and Max decided maybe she was human after all, and if she was, then she was within reach .... well, maybe. "I don't know whether you saw it or not, but she also had a bullet hole in the middle of her back," he said.

"She was shot too! This is so extraordinary!" Meg's eyes were very round. "And so peculiar!"

"I think I'd prefer that to beheading," Basil said. " I hate the thought of being dismembered." He grinned. "It offends my sense of order to think of having parts of me all scattered about."

"Are you both trying to make me sick?"

"Sorry," Basil said.

"Me too," Max said. It was one of those spaces in a conversation that usually he would have filled with some wonderfully insensitive remark, but instead he took a deep breath and let it out slowly. Not that he didn't think of one. He could have said, "nothing to lose your head over," or "if you keep your head when everyone around you is losing theirs, perhaps you don't understand the situation,' but he held it in because Meg wasn't putting on some girly act. She was genuinely upset. "The way I figure it," Max said, "they must not have been killed at the same time. But why would they throw one overboard and not the other?"

Basil shrugged. "Would it matter?"

"I don't know. I don't think she was beheaded on the boat because the only blood was in the cabin next to the body except for the trail the head left when it rolled away. But why would they do that?"

"Could you please be a little less graphic?" Meg asked.

"Sorry," Max said.

"But they still could have killed her on the boat."

"Right! All they had to do was wash down the deck."

"Maybe it was the Mafia," Basil said.

"Or some kind of drug thugs," Max said. "Maybe even someone else."

"Who?" Basil asked.

"Well, suppose ... "

Meg and Basil were sitting forward in their chairs now, alert and interested in the mystery, and suddenly their mother opened the door and stepped onto the porch. She wore white shorts and a blue silk blouse and it was pretty clear, Max thought, as he stood to greet her, where Meg got her looks.

"So," she said with a warm and genuine smile, "this must be the famous Mad Max Murphy, who this morning, I hear, saved countless numbers of children at West Wharf."

"Well, maybe eight or ten, anyway," Max said. "But all I did was shout and tell them to get off the beach. It wasn't very crowded."

"Oh, the story I heard was much more grand." She smiled and, like her daughter, she seemed to glow.

"It really wasn't a big deal," Max said.

"And I also understand that your family owns The Crab Trap where your father is at least a three-star chef?"

Max grinned, and the impish quality of it and direct way he looked at her caught her off guard. So did his words. "Dad's got plenty of stars, all right, but most of them are on the cognac bottles he uses in his cooking."

She laughed and reached out and shook his hand. "It's nice to meet you, Max."

And then he surprised her again. "The pleasure is mine, Lady Greene."

She appraised him carefully, clearly liking what she saw. He was certainly, she thought, a substantial cut above any American teenager she had met. He had charm and wit and she thought that Mad Max Murphy would hold his own in any company.

"Would you mind if I joined you for a minute? I want to hear all about what happened at West Wharf this morning, and in as much as you were Johnny on the spot, Max, you can offer an eyewitness account, and I always like to get things straight from the horse's mouth."

Max waited for her to sit and then sat back down.

Quickly he told her what had happened and then stopped, looked down and then back up as he shook his head. "Now it's even more peculiar," he said. "We found another body while we were out skiing."

"What?"

"It's true, Mother," Meg said. "Max spotted it and we put a marker on it and then he called his Uncle, who is the chief of police, and they came out and got it."

"How extraordinary!"

"Someone had lopped her head off as well," Basil said. "Can you imagine?"

"I rather wish I couldn't," Lady Greene said. "I don't suppose they have any idea what this is all about yet."

"I don't think so," Max said.

"Well, be sure and keep us apprised, if you can. I adore a good mystery, though I must admit it's a trifle disconcerting to have bodies popping up practically on one's doorstep." She rose and Max stood again, and for the first time in his life he thanked his mother for enforcing well-mannered behavior.

"It was a pleasure to meet you, Max, I hope we'll see more of you over the summer."

"I'm like a bad penny," Max said, "I always turn up."

They all laughed, and Max sat back down and picked up his soda.

"Smashing bit of work there, eh, Meg?" Basil asked.

"I think you've swept Mum off her feet. Such elegant manners." She smiled at him and this time there was no mistaking her curiosity, but what he liked best was the irony he saw there as well. Nobody would slide anything by Meg Greene.

"He even managed not to fawn and scrape like some

British toady," Basil said. "Impressive. Very impressive. Things in the colonies are looking up."

On such occasions it's hard to keep your feet under you, Max thought, but he simply smiled back. After all, the compliments here also carried some baggage. They were riding him just the least little bit, and the only question was whether it was all in good fun. For now he decided to take it that way and return fire. "You know, you chaps have simply got to adjust your language now that you're here. Sneak in a few local idioms and aphorisms, stuff like 'there's a many a good tune played on an old fiddle' and lose the 'Bob's your uncle' stuff."

It stopped them and they stared at him for a second, just long enough to catch the twinkle in his eye, and then they all laughed together.

"I've been thinking," Meg said. "What about spies? Could they have been spies of some kind? Perhaps this was a way to keep them quiet and warn others of what would happen if they talked."

"But they don't have to be spies," Max said.

"Anybody with something to cover up," Meg said. "Of course."

"What were you about to say when Mum came out?" Basil asked.

"What do you know about Plum Island?"

"Where's Plum Island?" Meg asked.

Max pointed out toward the water. "It's right out there, on the other side of the Sound. It sits just off Orient Point. The water between the island and the point is called Plum Gut. I've been there hundreds of times fishing.

"The government owns the island and officially it's a research facility for animal diseases, but everyone knows that they test all kinds of viruses and bacteria that could be used in germ warfare. Very secret. Very well guarded. And there have always been rumors about disease escaping the island. I know a guy, a naturalist I met one time when I was poking around in the marshes, and he said he was certain that Lyme disease came from there because the disease is carried on ticks, and the gulls that work the Sound fly back and forth all the time."

"I didn't know birds carried ticks," Basil said.

"Me either, but he said they do and Lyme is downwind of Plum Island in the summer."

"Oh my God," Meg said. "Do you suppose West Nile came from there too?"

"Why not. Birds carry the disease, don't they?" Basil had at last found something he could get his teeth into. Something solid and scientific, and that was by far his best subject. "The way it works, I think, is an infected bird could carry the disease and if it were bitten by a mosquito, then the mosquito could act as the vector. Or it could be that the mosquitos are the vector for both birds and humans."

Max grinned. "Vector?"

Meg interceded quickly. "Poor Basil's deeply into science," she said. "Sometimes I can't understand a word he says."

Basil was not easily thrown off. "It would be interesting to try proving that."

"Also kind of dangerous," Max said. "They've got bugs out there so vicious that a cup full could kill off everyone in the world."

"You don't say!"

Meg groaned. "God, Basil sometimes you sound like someone out of an old British movie."

He blushed. "Well, I can't see how, I mean ... "

Max knew enough about brothers and sisters to know that when one had the other on the ropes, they attacked. Meg, however did the exact opposite.

"Oh, I'm sorry, Basil, I shouldn't have said that. It was mean."

Basil grinned, still embarrassed but recovering. "No, you were absolutely right. We're in the U.S. now and I have to stop sounding so stuffy." He turned to Max. "I think it's left over from Eton. Everybody there spends most of their time trying to behave like nobility."

"No need to apologize to me," Max said.

"Well, all the same, please give me a boot in the backside if I do it again."

"How much more do you know about Plum Island?" Meg asked.

"Only what I told you."

"Do you think," Basil asked, "there's a chance the people out there might be involved?"

Max's cell phone went off and he punched the button and put it to his ear. "Hi. Sure. Right away. I've gotta get the boat back, can we meet there? Okay. Yup, thirty minutes at the most." He switched off the phone. "Gotta go," he said. "Uncle Carl wants to talk with me. Maybe I can find out what he knows so far."

"Will you tell us?" Meg asked.

"Sure. Maybe we can figure out something they can't."

"Is practice at the same time tomorrow?" Basil asked.

"One o'clock. Every day except on the weekends." Max picked up his glass and finished the soda. "See you tomorrow." He looked around at Meg and smiled. "Tomorrow?"

She smiled and nodded.

Six

The Brown Van

Carl helped Max drag the dinghy up the beach, and then carry the gear to the garage behind the cottage. He never dressed like a cop. He preferred khakis and boat shoes, though, to be sure, the shirt and pants had been starched and pressed. The shoes, however, were well worn and he topped himself with a blue baseball cap with the town seal on the front. Like most of the men in the family, his hair had thinned, but he was in very good shape and tanned from the time he spent fishing for blues and strip-ers, which was, after all, a family occupation. They all fished, and even his father found time to get away.

They stood next to Carl's dark green GMC pickup. "You headed home?" Carl asked.

"Yup."

"Throw your bike in the back. I'll give you a lift."

"I can live with that," Max said and he lifted the bike effortlessly over the side wall of the truck and set it gently on the bed.

"You been lifting weights?" Carl asked.

"Gymnastics and Tai Chi" Max said.

"So," Carl grinned. "You're a fighter too, huh?"

"Not me. I stay away from that stuff. Besides I wouldn't want to get in trouble with the cops."

Carl laughed. "Just like your father and me, huh?"

"You guys were fighters?"

"Let me put it this way. We never went looking for trouble."

They climbed into the truck. "So what's this with gymnastics? The school doesn't even have a team."

"It's for balance and agility. Those guys are the best at knowing where their body is. And you have to be strong from top to bottom. The Tai Chi is something else. Very strange stuff. I started last year. Mom got me into it. I just started the martial part of it a couple of months ago. You know how I always used to get ear infections? Well, since I started the Tai Chi I don't get them anymore."

Carl backed the truck around and headed up Harbor Avenue to Neck Road. "Kind of a busy day," he said.

"'It was the best of times, it was the worst of times ...'."

"What?"

"Dickens. From his novel on the French Revolution. Heads coming off in all directions."

Carl glanced around at his nephew and then back at the road, wondering what mixture of genes had turned up to make this most amazing young man. "Who were the kids with you?" he asked.

"Meg and Basil Greene."

Carl shook his head. "Heck of a thing to see. How did they react?"

"Okay, I think."

"Pretty horrible sight."

"The second one wasn't as bad," Max said. "No blood. And you couldn't see much."

"Did you notice anything else?"

"Like what?"

"Anything unusual."

Max shrugged. "I'm not real used to looking at bodies, but I can tell you this. She was missing her head."

"Did that bother you?"

"Yeah, a little, I guess. Maybe even more than that."

"How much more?"

Max grinned. "I've got a strong stomach."

"Twice in one day is a lot of headless horsemen."

"I'm okay."

"If you need to talk to somebody, let me know? We've got access to a shrink and he's pretty good."

"You send Grub to him yet?"

Carl grinned. "You don't miss much, do you?"

"Sometimes I wish I did. Now take your mother-in-law, for example." He told him about the encounter between Mrs. Santorini and the BMW.

"I'll talk to her," he said. "She's got it in her head that if somebody hits her, she'll be able to sue them."

"That's what Mom told me."

"Did you notice anything unusual besides the body?"

He looked around and grinned. "It's summer, Uncle Carl. The whole place is packed with crazy boat drivers cutting each other off, running aground, falling overboard. It's like a circus for screwups. And anyway, we were busy skiing. When I spotted the body there were no other boats in the area at all."

"How about this morning?"

"The first thing I noticed was the boat coming past the Surf Club at full throttle." He shifted in his seat. "You got any idea what this is all about?"

"Not a glimmer, Max. Not a glimmer. Except this. The boat was stolen. We don't even know who the guy was."

"I'll bet he was connected to something on Plum Island."

Carl groaned. "Oh, now don't start that stuff. Every time anything odd happens on the Sound, everyone blames the people on Plum. All we know is that two people turned up dead and we've got nothing to go on."

They turned onto Mungertown Road. "Where was the boat stolen from?"

"I'm supposed to be asking the questions here."

"Sorry. Just curious."

"Okay, I'll tell you that much. Port Jefferson."

"Why was the home port Westbrook?"

"We haven't been able to locate the owners yet."

"Where did they take the boat?"

"The Coast Guard towed it into New Haven."

"That's a pain. I'd like to look it over."

"Why?"

"I'm not sure. I keep thinking I saw something familiar but I can't make it come clear. I thought if I could look at the boat again it might help."

"Think it might be worth a trip to New Haven?"

"Worth a try."

"When?"

"Tomorrow morning. Early. I've got a driving lesson at ten and soccer practice at one."

Carl looked directly at him. "Max, just don't get any ideas about prying into this, okay? Remember, two people are dead, so whoever is doing this is very serious about eliminating anyone who might know something."

Max squirmed on the leather seat. "I won't say it didn't cross my mind."

"Well, forget about it, okay?" Carl turned into the driveway and drove around to the barn. "Max, you've got a reputation for doing things your own way. So far you've been lucky but this time you have to listen to me."

Max sighed. "Can I at least think about it?"

"Yeah, but that's all."

"Okay."

Carl took off his cap, smoothed his thin brown hair and screwed the cap back onto his head. "If you think of something let me know."

"Sure."

"Need a hand getting your bike out?"

"No. I can get it." Max climbed out of the truck, reached in and lifted his bike from the bed and then stood, holding the bike and looking at Carl still sitting in the cab. "About the body in the water. It looked to me like she'd been shot too."

"She had."

"Why do both?"

"To send a message, we think. They knew the body would turn up."

"Then why not leave her on the boat?"

"Good question."

"Maybe it was a hit."

"Certainly a possibility, but not the Mafia. They don't usually go in for that much blood."

"Do you think they'll find the woman's head?"

"Not likely. They tell me heads sink and stay there."

"Whoa, that's a weird thought; a human head just drifting around on the bottom, rolling back and forth with the tides."

"In any case, not a pretty thought. I wouldn't spend too much time thinking about that if I were you, Max."

"Good call," Max said. Then he shook his head. "There sure was a lot of blood."

"Seven a.m. tomorrow, okay?"

"Sure."

"See you then."

Max rolled his bike into the barn and locked it to the wall as he had since Wayne's bike had been stolen several years ago.

Max walked into the kitchen. "Hi, Mom, what's for supper?"

"Why did Uncle Carl drive you home?" His mother stood at the stove, watching what looked like pieces of breaded chicken slowly browning in a big skillet.

"What's that?" Max looked into the frying pan.

"A new recipe I'm trying."

"Guinea pig Max gets to preview another menu item."

Several inches shorter than her son, slender with pale blue eyes and brown hair pulled back into a pony tail, his mother grinned. "Think it'll kill you?"

He looked into the pan and in truth it looked very tasty and it sure smelled good. "Probably not. Do you think you made enough?"

"It's a recipe for four."

He nodded. "Should be enough."

"Now, why did Carl drive you home?

"Found another body." He opened the refrigerator door and began his usual inventory of the contents.

"Another body!"

"A woman. Most of her was drifting just this side of Hammonasset."

"What? Most of her?"

"Another case of a missing head."

"Max, close the door. And don't fill up on snacks. And tell me more about this!"

He raised his head and sniffed the air. "I just happened to see something floating and I called Uncle Carl."

"My God, this is terrible!"

He looked at the skillet. "Smells good."

"Not the food. The murders."

"Pretty nasty," Max said as he looked into the frying pan. "Are those dried tomatoes?"

"They are. And I still don't understand why you won't eat at the restaurant," she said.

"'Cause I don't live there. I've told you that." He closed the refrigerator and walked to the pantry, grabbed the can of red peanuts, and carried it to the table. "Besides, this way you get to try out new recipes on someone other than the help."

"Tell me about the body."

"She'd also been shot in the back. Definitely murder. I'm going with Uncle Carl tomorrow morning to look at the boat."

"What's wrong with our boat?"

"Not our boat, the boat that ran up onto the beach."

"Why?"

"I think I saw something, but I can't think what it is."

"Don't eat any more peanuts."

He sniffed the air again. "That isn't chicken."

"How could you possibly tell."

"I'm guessing ostrich."

She looked into the pan and then at her son. "How could you guess that? Of all the birds there are in the world, why would you guess ostrich?"

"It's perfectly logical, Mom. The ostrich guys are trying to market their product and you're always looking for something to set the restaurant apart."

She sighed. How could he be so smart and get such mediocre grades? "Who did you go skiing with?"

"I told you, Basil Greene. His sister Meg came too. She is a great skier. They're new in town."

"You did tell me that, didn't you. Only I didn't make the connection. Aren't they Lord and Lady Greenes' children?"

It sounded odd to hear them referred to that way and just as odd to hear them called "children." They weren't children. Or were they? What did the word actually mean? Wouldn't they always be Lord and Lady Greene's children? "Yup." He said, "Basil's playing soccer. He's pretty cool. Talks funny, though."

"You'll get used to that." She grinned. "What'd you think of Meg?"

It stopped him cold. Dangerous question. Don't give her anything to go on here, he thought. "She's nice."

"Knockout is more like it."

"Yup. That too."

"Is that all I get? A yup?"

"Mom, I think you need a reality check here. She's the daughter of the tenth Earl of Harrowfield."

"You think you're not good enough, is that it?"

There were plenty of things not to like about parents, but most of them you could ignore. Pushiness on subjects like this was not of one of them. Because anything he said here might reveal the way he felt about Meg and he was definitely not going there.

"We met them at The Trap last week. They were with Professor Zales and his wife. They seemed really down to earth, Max."

"They are. Basil's a terrific soccer player. He was all-prep at Choate."

She turned from the stove and stared at him, "Max, you're making me crazy here. What about Meg?"

"We were secretly married last night."

All she could do was laugh. "Okay, rat, I get the hint. Boys don't talk about stuff like this with their mothers, right?"

He grinned. "Right." But she knew how he felt, and he thought that in the future he would simply have to find a new tactic to throw her off. The question was what? Mothers, after all, are female and all females are into relationships. It made his skin feel wormy just thinking about it ... not Meg, but talking about her with his mother. Ugh! Gross! Not what he had in mind, even if he wasn't sure just what he did have in mind.

From the window he could see the street and he watched a brown commercial type van cruise slowly past. The heavily tinted windows prevented seeing the driver and the van was nondescript except for the magnetic sign on the side, which said, "Brett's Chimney Cleaning." There was also a long scratch in the paint along the rocker panel as if it had brushed against a big stone. As always, he recorded detail and stored it away. He was known for that in the family. He simply saw things other people did not. Partly, that came from having exceptional eyesight; twenty/five at his last checkup, but he also had a photographic memory so that what he saw stayed with him for a long, long time. The only shortcoming he'd encountered was not always being able to put each bit of information into a context which allowed him to recall it quickly. What he needed was access codes like the ones used to pull information from a computer.

He had noticed over the past year or so, however, that he was getting better at that, and more and more he could pull things out of his memory when he needed them. In an odd way that also turned out to be somewhat frustrating because no one in the family remembered things as accurately as he did. It wasn't that they didn't remember, but that they could never recall details exactly as they had appeared.

That, of course led to another interesting question. How much did memory change the details of what had happened in order to make you more comfortable?

And then another question arose. Why did some things command attention while others did not? Like the van. Why had he noticed it? Because of the murders? Had that made him especially suspicious? Certainly it hadn't been the van itself. There were thousands of such vans driven by craftsmen. And yet something about it had caught his eye, maybe because it was going so slowly, maybe that's why he had noticed it, but he was pretty sure it was something else. He shrugged it off. It would either connect or it would not and there was no sense in torturing himself over it, though he knew he would until he had a logical explanation.

"What was all that stuff the UPS guy dropped off?"

"I told you, Mom. It's for my hydrogen generator."

"What? You're going into the bomb business?"

She sounded pretty much alarmed, he thought. "Mom,

we're not talking weapons grade plutonium here. We're talking hydrogen gas to burn in the furnace or in any internal combustion engine."

"And your father okayed this? It sounds dangerous."

Max shook his head. "Not dangerous."

"Wasn't it hydrogen that blew up the Hindenberg?" She turned to look at him over her glasses. "Hydrogen gas, as I recall."

"Yup. But that was free gas and the gas I use is absorbed in a medium which is in propane tanks and once the medium absorbs the gas it can only be released at a given rate so the most it can do is burn."

"You're losing me here, Max."

"Forget the science part."

"Isn't that the part that blows up?"

Max groaned. "Mom … it won't blow up. Trust me."

But his mother looked more doubtful by the second. "Have you checked this out with your father?"

"Of course. You think I'd do something like this without telling him?" He was on treacherous ground. He had only told his father that he was working on a project for next year's state science fair, using electrolysis to break down water. He had left out the part about the hydrogen. "Besides, how'd you like to heat the house this winter for nothing?"

"Okay, I know when I'm being had."

"You'll see. I'll heat the house and I'll win the state science fair."

"How much is this project likely to cost?"

"I haven't got any idea. I think the biggest expense will be renting a Ditch Witch to bury the fuel line in from the barn."

"And you're paying for all of this, right?"

"No way. I haven't got any money."

"Write me a proposal and list what you've spent so far, then show me how much more you're likely to spend."

Good old Mom, always a number cruncher. But that was no bad thing when you considered that her constant monitoring kept the business profitable.

What he did was agree. After all, she hadn't said when he had to give her the proposal.

"Okay. Wash up and let's eat."

He walked out of the kitchen and into the back hall and then down to the bathroom, thinking about setting up the hydrogen generator. With any luck he'd have it ready to go in a couple of days. He already had a dozen old propane tanks and Mr. Ucello had promised him that many more again, as he took them out of circulation. It simplified matters greatly that they already heated with gas. But the big question, the one he could not answer without some help from Mr. Ucello, who, it turned out, had a clear interest in the project because he did, after all, run a propane business, was just how many cubic feet of gas it would take to heat the house for an hour during the winter.

He dried his hands and headed for the kitchen. It was going to be a great summer. He had something to work on, he'd made some new friends, he was the only goalie, and he even had a double murder to solve. Things had never looked better.

Seven

Negotiating With Adults

Max stepped down onto the yacht from the Coast Guard pier, opened the door, and walked into the cabin. The body and the head were gone but the blood had dried on the carpet in wide dark stains.

Carl followed him into the cabin. "Look a little different?"

"Oh, yeah. A lot different with the body gone." He shook his head. "I don't think I'm gonna be much help."

"Let your eyes roam. Walk around."

Max began by walking back to the door. He stood and looked around and then pointed to a door on his left, walked over and opened it and looked inside. It was the head. "This door was open," he said.

"I'll have them check the holding tank. Maybe somebody got rid of something."

"Like drugs?"

"Not very effective on a boat with a holding tank," Carl said and then shrugged. "But it's worth a try."

Max began walking around the cabin, doing just what Uncle Carl had said, letting his eyes sweep slowly, hoping that something would click. He stopped at the helm, picked up a small metal flashlight and absently, as he did with every flashlight, switched it on. The batteries were dead. Pretty sloppy. On a boat you always checked the lights. He set it back on the small counter behind the wheel and the flashlight rolled forward and dropped into the shallow well designed to catch any condensation from the glass above. It was like it had fallen off the edge of the world. He thought about reaching for it so he could put it back where he'd found it and then shrugged. What difference would it make? And anyway, the batteries were dead.

He scratched his head. "Did you find out who he was yet?"

Carl grunted. "He was a marine biologist and he ran a small company that did evaluations of property that other companies wanted to build on. George Waterstreet, age 49, five-nine, brown hair, blue eyes, Ph.D. in marine biology. Married and divorced, two kids, both in college."

"Where did he come from?"

"He lived in Sag Harbor. His company was there too. Clean record. Not even a traffic ticket. The company had done very well. Made a lot of money."

"Who owns the boat?"

"Robert Chase, of Port Jefferson. He had just bought a place in Madison and the home port on the boat had just been repainted."

"For Westbrook."

"Right."

Max looked around, absorbing every detail, but nothing connected. "Did his company have a boat?"

"No idea. Probably. It would fit with their line of work."

"I guess I've seen enough," Max said. "Maybe it was something about the body. Sorry I wasn't more help."

Carl grinned and clapped him on the shoulder. "It'd been anyone else, Max, I wouldn't have made the trip. You've got kind of a strange reputation, you know."

Max nodded. "Yeah, I know, but I'm not sure it's worth being known as weird."

They stepped outside and Max stopped and looked at the teak bulkhead that divided the cabin from the after deck. Something out of place caught his eye and Max stopped and scanned back over the finely finished wood. What he'd seen was a tiny splinter up under the lower edge of the molding which joined the wood to the fiberglass above. He stepped closer, reached up, ran his index finger over the small spot. Then he pointed to a hole in the wood. "Looks like a bullet hole, maybe a twenty-two."

Carl stepped closer. "Sure does." He took out his pocket knife and cut into the wood around the hole, careful not to let the blade get too close to the edges to prevent any damage to the bullet. It took several minutes but finally he extracted the small lump of lead. "I'll have the crime lab run this through. If it came from a gun used in a crime, it may turn up." He grinned. "They're gonna be a little embarrassed, though. They went over this boat with a fine-toothed comb." He pulled a small plastic bag from his shirt pocket, dropped the bullet into it, and slipped the bag back into the pocket.

"Are you doing the investigation?" Max asked.

"The jurisdiction is a little complicated. The body was found on land only because the boat came ashore. But the murder was out at sea so the FBI and the state police get this one, along with the Coast Guard and the DEA. But all of that won't stop me from nosing around. Sometimes the local guy just knows where to look."

"Sounds more than a little complicated," Max said.

They climbed into the truck. "I'd give odds this goes nowhere," Carl said.

"Too many cooks in the pot end up mashing the vegetables," Max said.

Carl laughed. "Where do you come up with that stuff?"

"It just pops into my head."

"Like solving a murder has?"

"What can I do? I don't have a crime lab. I don't know how to conduct an investigation. I don't know anything."

"It's not working, Max. I know you too well." He sighed. "I wasn't going to tell you this but maybe you better hear it." He took a deep breath. "Before they cut the guy's head off they tortured him. Terrible stuff. Pulled his fingernails, then they broke his fingers and his toes and finally his arms and his legs. Then they killed him which means either he talked and they didn't need him anymore or he didn't talk and they gave up and had to get rid of a witness. Whoever these guys are, Max, they play for keeps."

For awhile Max said nothing and then finally he nodded. "Okay," he said. "I got the message."

"I hope you mean that, Max."

They rode in silence for some time and finally Carl spoke. "Is Jenks coaching the team this summer?"

"Yup."

"Think you'll play much?"

"I'm the only goalie."

"Yeah, but can you stop anything?"

Max grinned at the friendly gibe. "Everything," he said,

"well, almost everything."

☞   ☞   ☞

His driving instructor showed up right on the dot at ten. She was precise and she demanded perfection. Mrs. Gewurtzenheimer was also a large woman, with nearly white blond hair and razor sharp blue eyes.

Usually, Max could have slipped his mooring and drifted, just gone with the flow. But he just couldn't seem to get past the fact that Mrs. Gewurtzenheimer had a death grip on his future. You did it the way she said or you didn't pass and that meant you couldn't take the test with the state.

So it was with some trepidation that Max walked out to the car, climbed in, said good morning, and buckled himself into the driver's seat.

He felt like an airline pilot running through the check list on a 747 as he fastened his eyes on the dials and gauges and made sure he knew what every switch and button meant.

"Today we will spend some time on the turnpike," she said. "Do you know how to get there?"

He'd heard dumber questions, he thought, but outside of the questions in health class, he couldn't think where. Of course he knew how to get there. You turned left at the end of the driveway and then you ... then you ... his mind had gone blank. Did you go left or right? When they went into New Haven which way did they turn?

He felt several beads of sweat slip down his sides beneath his tee shirt. Never had he felt so stupid.

"Go down to Greenhill and turn right," she said. Her voice seemed to fill the car. "Now remember. When you turn the wheel, the car should be fully stopped."

"Okay," Max said. It wasn't what his father had taught him. You never turned the wheel unless you started in motion, especially on pavement. It shortened the life of the tires. He was not, however, about to argue.

He slowed coming up to the stop sign and checked in both directions and then turned right.

"Aha!" she said as she marked something on the paper attached to her clipboard. "A rolling stop. One point deduction."

Max cursed silently. How could he have done that? He knew you were supposed to come to a full stop. Okay, he told himself, concentrate. A short way down the road they came to a sharp curve to the left and Max slowed to below the speed limit and let the car find its way around the turn.

"Aha!" Mrs. Gewurtzenheimer said. "Minus one point for letting the car come too close to the centerline of the road."

"But I was inside the line," Max said. "I was on my side of the road."

"Too close. You could make an oncoming driver nervous. You never know who's driving. It could be a mother with a child and she might think you were going to cross into her lane and she would drive off the road."

"Yes, Ma'am," Max said.

At Route 1 he came to a full stop. He had no choice. The traffic was heavy and he had to wait for an opening.

Once he had pulled out, she nodded. "Good," she said, "You could have gone sooner, but it's always better to be on the safe side."

Sooner? When? "I thought it was too close," he said.

"No. After the third car went past you had enough

space."

She was totally nuts. If he'd pulled out, the guy in the other car would have had to slow way down. If the guy had been going the speed limit, it would have been okay, but at the speed he'd been traveling it would have been a close call. It wasn't just a matter of how far away the car had been, but how fast it was going.

At Goose Lane they turned up onto the turnpike. Max remembered to use his signal light each time and he kept the car right at the speed limit.

"As you pull up onto the turnpike you'll have to merge with the oncoming traffic. Give yourself plenty of space and then pull in."

He did it the way his father had taught him. As he started into the merge lane he accelerated until he reached the speed of the cars coming up from behind, and then adjusted his speed slightly to allow himself to merge seamlessly with the traffic.

"Aha! Minus one point. Travelling too fast on a ramp."

"I had to get up to speed to merge," Max said.

"No. The ramp speed is forty."

"But the cars on the turnpike are traveling over sixty-five. I needed to be going the same speed to merge."

"All you have to do is put on your signal light so they let you in."

"Don't they have the right of way?"

"They're supposed to let you merge," she said.

He said no more, concentrating on driving. It was much easier on the turnpike. All you had to do was stay in your lane and drive at the speed limit. They drove to Branford and then got off.

Getting back onto the turnpike to head home, Max did

exactly as she told him and as a result pulled out into the traffic at forty miles an hour causing the driver behind him to have to slow because there wasn't time to get up to speed before the car was on his bumper. The guy blew his horn and made a series of obscene gestures.

"Ignore that. It's called road rage. He had plenty of time to change lanes."

Max just kept on driving. There had been no place for the guy to go because the traffic in the left hand lane had not a single break as far back as he could see. Which meant that the guy behind him was not a happy camper because Max drove at fifty-five, right on the speed limit, while the traffic to his left blew past at close to seventy.

His lane was empty for as far ahead as he could see and behind him the traffic was solid, also as far as he could see. Maybe it would be better, he thought, if they kept student drivers off the turnpike because right now he was pissing off more people at once than he had in his whole life.

☞   ☞   ☞

Dad was up by the time he got back and he found him out in the barn looking over the equipment. He was the same height as Uncle Carl but he needed to lose about fifteen pounds. That would have meant no longer tasting what he cooked and giving up sampling the food was next to impossible.

"Heck of a bunch of stuff you got here, Max," he said.

"I'll need a lot more tanks, though."

"You think this is gonna work?"

"Sure. I got it all figured out."

His father grinned at him and shook his head. "You

never have suffered from a lack of confidence." He pointed to the boxes UPS had brought the day before. "What's in the boxes?"

"The parts for the generator."

"How does it work?"

"You send an electric current into water and it ..."

"Whoa! Wait a minute here. Electricity into water? That's the way people get electrocuted."

"It's okay, Dad, honest. I got a set of plans from Dr. Plonsky at UConn. And he told me where to get the equipment and the plans show how to do everything without any danger. And Mr. Ucello said he'll install the new gas line to the furnace. He's been a big help. He supplied all the tanks and he located a place to get the aluminum hydride to put into the tanks so the hydrogen can't explode."

Tom Murphy stood with his hands in his pockets as Max explained in Max fashion just what he was up to. He talked at lightening speed, waving his hands, and jumping around like a grasshopper.

"The way it works, I set up the hydrogen generator out on the lawn in a shed and then I use an array of solar cells to generate a current which breaks down the water into hydrogen and oxygen. The oxygen comes off on one side and the hydrogen on the other. The oxygen is pumped away in a long pipe and the hydrogen goes into the tanks with the hydride. Those tanks get connected to the furnace. In order to make the hydride release the hydrogen, the tanks have to be heated so I'll put a heating coil in the tanks which will tap into the hot water system. I'll use enough propane to get the water up to temperature and then shut off the propane and use the hydrogen. And because I use solar cells to produce the hydrogen, the whole system is pretty close to free. The reason I need so many tanks is to make sure we have gas on hand to get through the darker part of the year when I won't have enough sunlight to generate large amounts of gas. I still have some things to work out, of course, but Dr. Plonsky said I can call him anytime and Mr. Ucello is really interested too."

"If this is so easy, how come everyone isn't doing it?"

Max shrugged. "I don't know. Part of it is the tanks. Once they're loaded with the hydride, they're pretty heavy." He grinned. "What's neat is that generating hydrogen is like having your own oil well. Even better, because this fuel doesn't need to be refined. It's pure from the start and when you burn it, the only by-products are heat and water. And think about this! The supply is endless."

Tom shook his head and smiled at his son. "How are you doing for cash here?"

"Well, I was gonna ask you about that."

"Have you got a budget?"

"You mean for the whole project?"

"Yup."

"Not exactly." How did they do it, he wondered? They must have talked about it. "I mean, I don't have a budget. I've just been buying what I need with the money I was saving up to buy a car. I've just about used that up but I still have to buy the aluminum hydride, and it won't be cheap and I'll need a truckload."

"How expensive?"

"I haven't got any idea."

"Well, how about I talk to Pete Ucello and I'll work out something with him. I'll show you how to set up a budget too. If you're gonna do this, you might as well do it right, and budgeting correctly is the way you make a business profitable. The only way you can properly price what you sell is to know how much it cost you to make it. We do that every week at the Trap. Thanks to your mother, I always know how much I can spend on supplies and how much I'll have to charge. It's not just good business, it's the only way to run a business.

"Don't look so crestfallen. If you're gonna do something, you need to do it the right way. Com'on inside. I'm gonna get a cup of coffee and we can talk some more and maybe you can tell me more about what happened yesterday. Have you seen this morning's paper?"

They walked toward the house. "I'm in the paper?"

"From what they say, you're something of a hero."

"Me?"

"Yeah. The people on the beach all said if you hadn't warned them someone would have been killed for sure."

"Wow ..." Max shook his head. "All I did was holler. Nothing very heroic about that."

"And what if you hadn't hollered?"

Max shrugged. "I hadn't thought about it."

"Would the boat have run into someone?"

"I don't know. I mean, sooner or later they would have heard it or seen it."

"But nobody had by the time you warned them, right?"

"I always thought of a hero as someone like Pele."

"Pele wasn't a hero. He was an idol. Heroes act to help others, usually without ever worrying about the danger to themselves."

Max grinned. "Not me, then. I got out of there as fast as I could. Good thing I did too. The boat pretty well mutilated Mom's favorite beach chair."

"Uh-oh. Have you told her yet?"

"Not yet."

"Want me to tell her?"

"No. I'll tell her," Max said, but he did not sound happy.

"Not to worry on this one, Max. In a choice between you and the beach chair, I'd guess she'd give up the beach chair without a thought."

"You think?"

"Absolutely. You're worth a lot more than a beach chair."

They both laughed as they headed into the kitchen for a cup of coffee.

Eight

Suddenly He Remembers

After lunch Max hopped onto his Cannondale and headed for soccer practice. It wasn't cool to bike but Max didn't care what anyone thought. He liked riding fast and it was great for his legs and if there was one thing a soccer player had to have it was powerful legs.

For a good rider with a fast bike it wasn't much of a ride, just a few miles, and he'd have been there well ahead of time if he hadn't come up behind a tractor trailer on Mungertown Road. The guy took up so much space that it just wasn't safe to try and get past him.

What was he doing here anyway? There was no way he could get under the railroad bridge. He should have turned off at Greenhill. Max grinned. This ... was gonna be worth watching. Not that it hadn't happened before, because any number of trucks had tried to get under the bridge and gotten stuck, but most of them had been crawling along and this guy was going close to thirty.

Max stopped and watched as the truck headed down

the low hill to the underpass. The guy must be on drugs, Max thought as he watched him run his trailer smack into the bridge, the metal peeling back, squealing like Mr. Walton's piglets the time the coyote had gotten into the pen.

The truck finally came to a stop and Max pushed off and started downhill to pass him and then had to grab his brakes as a woman in a Suburban, coming from the opposite way, decided to go between the truck and the left hand wall of the underpass. The sound this time had more of a scraping quality to it as the passage narrowed and she managed to jam the Suburban like a cork in a bottle between the wall and the side of the truck.

Max reached for his cell phone.

"Hello, Mrs. Field, it's Max Murphy. Is Uncle Carl there?"

"I'm sorry, he's busy and can't possibly be interrupted."

"Late lunch, huh?"

"Max, you can't just call here and bother your uncle. He is the chief of police and he is a very busy man."

"And he's gonna be busier still," Max said.

In the background he heard Uncle Carl say; "Is that Max?"

"Yes, chief."

"I'll take it — Max?"

"Uncle Carl, I think you better send a bunch of people over to the Mungertown railroad bridge. There's a semi jammed under it and some woman in a Suburban tried to squeeze past and now she's stuck too. All her doors are jammed and she's got a couple of kids in the car and now the truck driver can't get out either."

"And you're the witness, of course?"

"Yeah, but I'm leaving. I've got soccer practice. I'll give you a statement later, okay?"

"Grub's nearby. Hold on a second." He could hear Uncle Carl on the radio and then he came back to the phone. "He's on his way."

"You're gonna need a big wrecker and a cutting torch."

"That bad, huh?"

"Whoa! The driver just got out through his window and now he's dancing around on the hood of the Suburban like an absolute madman, and the woman inside looks a little panicky."

"What the hell gets into people? Every day gets stranger and stranger. Max, tell the driver to calm down, will you. I don't want this to get out of hand."

"I don't think he's gonna listen, Uncle Carl. Maybe you'll need some extra guys and a straight jac ... Whoa! He just lost his footing and fell off the Suburban. Guess you better call the EMTs too. I think he hit his head. I can hear Grub's siren. I'll tell him what happened and then I gotta go."

"Good, good. I've got more people on their way."

But Grub pulled up on the other side of the bridge and there was no way to get there other than to climb the embankment and cross the tracks, and with the new high-speed trains running, that just was not an option.

He walked past the truck driver, sitting on the road holding his head with both hands and moaning. Max climbed up onto the bumper of the Suburban. The woman looked at him as if he had wandered out of a darkened graveyard. "It's gonna be okay," Max called. He could hear the kids in the back seat crying. "The cops are here and more help is on the way."

As high as he stretched he couldn't see Grub, so he

climbed onto the well-dented hood. Grub was just getting out of the cruiser.

"Sergeant Grub! There's a man over here who's hurt. See if you can open the back door of the Suburban and help the people out. I can't stay, I have to get to practice."

Grub peered at him over the roof of the Suburban. "What are you doing up there? Can't you see there's been an accident? Get down from there!"

Max shook his head. "Just help the people out the back of the Suburban, okay?"

"Hey, kid, get off of there. I got a job to do and you're interfering with the police."

How could anyone be that dumb, Max thought as he climbed down.

"Oh, my head ... " the driver groaned.

Max looked down at him. "Hey, you wanna dance you gotta pay the piper," he said and then walked to his bike, jumped on, and headed for practice. He was late and nothing made a coach angrier.

In fact, he was ten minutes late getting there but that wasn't the worst part. Watkins was standing in the goal. Max laid his bike down and walked onto the field.

"Sorry I'm late, Coach," he said. "There was an accident and I had to stay till the cops got there."

He smiled broadly. "No problem, Max. Did you see who turned up? I talked to his boss at Munger Lumber and he gave Watkins time off to practice."

Max nodded. "Gee, thanks," he said.

"You'll be playing back-up now that Watkins's here."

"Why would you start a second rate goalie?" Max asked.

"Who? Watkins? Watkins' is a great goalie. You need to

watch the way he plays."

Max watched a skinny little freshman drive a shot into the net. "Like that one?"

"He's just warming up."

Max shook his head and walked down to stand behind the goal to wait his turn. He waved to Basil and then leaned against the goal post, watching shot after shot fly into the net. With Watkins in goal the rest of the teams in the league would wipe the floor with them. He was pissed, majorly pissed, but all he could do was wait his turn and finally, when he stepped into the goal, he stopped every single shot, even Basil's best. But it made no difference. He was back to second string goalie and now he had to make a decision. If he quit he would never make the high school team in the fall. If he stayed, he'd make the team and sit on the bench hoping that Watkins got injured.

At the break Watkins came up behind him. "Think you're pretty hot with all that crazy diving around, don't you, Murphy?"

"Sure beats what you did. What are you trying out for, the International Zombies?"

Watkins poked him in the chest with his right index finger. He was at least two inches taller and probably twenty pounds heavier, but poking Max was a bad idea. Before you could blink, Max grabbed onto his finger and bent it back into his hand, then twisted his arm around behind his back. "Don't ever do that again, Watkins, or I'll tear your finger out by the roots." He let go and looked around but as far as he could tell no one had seen him.

"You're crazy, you know that! You are really crazy! Do you know what I could have done to you?"

Max laughed. "Well go ahead and do it. I'm just standing here waiting. You're what, two years older and bigger and fatter, so go ahead, make a move."

"And get in trouble with the Coach? Not a chance. But don't think you're getting away with this. I got a lot of friends, you know."

"And you're gonna tell those friends that you, a senior, need their help against a sophomore?" Max laughed again, trying to goad him into losing his temper, but it didn't work.

"Just remember, I'll be looking for you."

"I'm easy to find."

As he watched Watkins walk away, Max thought of another option. He could play for someone else. Nothing said he had to play for Madison. Why not try Guilford or Clinton? And he knew Guilford was practicing this afternoon and their goalie from last year had graduated. The only goalie they had coming up was in the same league with Watkins. Besides he had something of an in with the coach there.

He trotted off the field and walked over to Basil as they took a break.

"Not much of a goalie," Basil said.

"Yeah."

"But he's going to get all the time, isn't he?"

"That's the way Jenks does it."

"This team is in trouble. The defensemen are quite hopeless and this guy Watkins can't stop anything. With you in goal we at least had a chance."

"I'm quitting," Max said.

"Then I'm quitting too," Basil said. "I'd rather not play than play for a rotter like Jenks."

Max looked around at him. "I got a plan," he said.

"Oh?" Basil's eyes widened.

"I'm gonna go see if I can play for Guilford."

"I thought you played for the town where you lived?"

"That's what everybody thinks, but it's not true. If it were, none of the summer kids could play."

"When are you going?"

Max walked over and picked up his bike. "Their practice starts at two-thirty."

"Can you get there in time?"

"Dunk shot."

"Next thing I know you'll be entering the Tour de France."

Max swung his leg over the frame of the bike. "I'll call you later and let you know how it comes out. I'm thinking they could use an all-prep striker too."

"Do you know the coach?"

Max grinned. "Who, Uncle John?"

"My God, this place is like an ingrown toenail. Is everyone related?"

"The Murphys and the Cardwells all come from large families."

"Let me know how it turns out."

"Of course."

☞   ☞   ☞

Max was sitting on the bench when Uncle John Cardwell pulled up in his battered old pickup, the bed nearly overflowing with lobster pots and buoys. He was the youngest of the uncles, still in his twenties, still a bachelor but the story in the family said that was because he was so good looking that women couldn't leave him alone. But nobody seemed to resent it, perhaps in part because Uncle John never made anything of it. He never talked about it, he never boasted, he just went out for lobsters and in the afternoons he showed up at The Trap for a couple of beers.

"Hey, Max, what are you doing here? You lost? This is Guilford."

"You need a goalie?"

"Here's something different. A guy from Madison wants to play goal for a Guilford team?"

"You know Jenks, right?"

"Sure I know him. Don't like him, but I know him."

"Well, he's got Watkins in goal and there's no chance I'll get to play unless somebody breaks his legs, and hey, I've done a few rotten things now and then, but I'm definitely not into breaking somebody's legs."

"So you want to try out here?"

"Right."

"No favorites, Max."

"I can beat out Waller any time."

"I got a summer kid too. Could be a sleeper."

Max grinned. "I don't mind competition as long as I get a fair chance to compete."

"Fair enough."

"How are you set at striker?"

"Weak. Very weak."

"How about an all-prep striker from Choate?"

"Basil Greene?"

"You know him?"

"I saw him play."

"Where?"

"At Choate."

"What were you doing there?"

"The marine biology guy asked me to talk about the state of the Sound and as I was leaving there was a game and I never pass up the chance to watch a game." He reached into the back of his truck and pulled out a bag full of soccer balls. "So what's the story?"

"He doesn't think much of Jenks either."

"This day just gets better and better."

"He'll be here tomorrow."

"We're gonna be short handed for a couple of weeks. All the best players are up at soccer camp at UConn. Everybody wants to play for Ray Reid. That's what an NCAA championship does for you."

"He's a great coach."

"The best. I played for him when he was at Southern and we won the NCAA's. The guy's a magician, Max."

Slowly, other players began to arrive, hopping out of Volvos and BMWs and upscale SUVs. And while Max lived in the next town to the east, his reputation had spread far and wide. Sometimes it seemed as if a new Mad Max story surfaced every day.

But these kids were all new and none of them knew he was related to the coach.

The first two goalies worked out ahead of him, and Max began to breath a little easier. The summer kid was good enough, but he needed a season or two more. Waller was a total rookie.

When his turn came, Max started slowly, just stopping each shot with no apparent effort. But then they didn't have much in the way of scorers either. Once inside the box, though, anyone can score. But not against me, Max thought, as he dove to his right and flicked the ball away. If he didn't give them the full show it was because he didn't need to.

At the end he felt sort of bad that he'd taken the position away from the other goalies, but there was bound to be a game where they'd get some time and he decided to make it clear to Uncle John that he ought to play them when he could.

On the way home he stopped at The Trap for a soda and sat out back drinking it and thinking about what kind of a team they were gonna have and then he remembered. The guy on the boat had been wearing a lapel pin; a little gold pin with a red bulls-eye. And the guy in the red BMW who'd tangled with Mrs. Santorini had been wearing a pin just like it. What did that mean? Some kind of secret group? He finished his soda, carried the can around to the recycling bin on the east side of the building by the dumpster, and then headed home. He had a phone call to make and maybe he could check the Internet and see what he could dig up.

"Basil? It's Max."

"What did you find out?"

"Guilford needs a striker really bad. In fact, they need players at every position until some of the varsity guys get back from soccer camp. Uncle John would love to have you play for him. What happened after I left?"

"Jenks gave us a big speech on being a quitter and that's about it. He's rather a bad coach, you know."

"Yeah, I know. But it doesn't matter, because after this he'll never play me. Not that he was gonna play me anyway, but it's gonna make school pretty dull without having soccer to look forward to." He sighed. "You pays your money and you takes your chances."

"Mother asked me to ask you if you would like to come to dinner tonight."

It caught him by surprise but there was only one way to answer. "Sure. What time?"

"We eat at seven, but why don't you get here early so we can chat a bit."

Max grinned. He was beginning to like the way Basil talked. "Five-thirty okay?"

"Perfect. Meg's got a friend here from school, so it ought to be fun."

His heart sank. She had a boyfriend. Damn! Sometimes he thought if it weren't for bad luck he wouldn't have any luck at all. "Okay then, see you at five-thirty. And thanks."

"My pleasure."

He went back to his computer, searching through every environmental site he could find but he didn't turn up a single insignia that resembled that lapel pin. Max shut down his computer and headed downstairs and out to the huge herb garden where his mother was gathering an assortment of herbs for the restaurant.

"Mom, can you drive me over to Basil's at about five-fifteen? I've been invited to dinner."

"Of course." She stood up, her eyes wide. "I hope they don't expect you to dress for dinner."

Max grinned. "Well, turning up naked is probably not what they had in mind."

She laughed. "No, I don't think so either. Dress for dinner means black tie, usually, or at the least, coat and tie."

"No way am I wearing a coat and tie just to eat. It's summer and in summer I wear shorts, a tee shirt, and my Topsiders and that's it. "

"But Max, you don't want to embarrass yourself, do you?"

He shrugged. "I won't be embarrassed."

"You've got some nice polo shirts. At least wear one of those. And you've those great looking shorts you got from Bean's." Suddenly she looked almost defiant. "This is

America, after all, and in a shore town in America, in the summer, that's the way people dress."

"Yeah, go Mom!"

She smiled at him. "Do as the Romans do, and this is Rome."

"I'm glad that's settled," Max said. "*Omnia fundabulus vincit.*"

"What does that mean?"

He shrugged. "Nothing, but you'd have to know Latin to know that, and nobody knows any Latin anymore."

Nine

A Pleasant Surprise

Max spent the rest of the afternoon working on his hydrogen generator, setting up the pieces as Dr. Plonsky had described. But it was hard to concentrate. He set the tools aside and left the barn, walking up to the house, and flopping onto one of the chaise lounges on the deck. Who was this guy Meg had invited? Her boyfriend? Who else? Damn, but he hated stuff like this. It was so stupid to sit here worrying about whether she had a boyfriend. Of course she had a boyfriend. Any girl who looked like Meg Greene had boys following up her wake like albacore chasing bait.

And why should it bother him that she was going out with some rich kid from private school, some senior, probably from Greenwich or New Canaan. And you could be sure he'd be driving a Porsche. All those guys drove Porsches. And they wore Rolexes too. And they lived in monster trophy houses and ... and he was really being stupid about this. Basil and Meg lived in one of those houses but they didn't wear Rolex watches or drive Porsches. And he knew plenty of kids who summered here who went to private schools and they were as easy to get along with as any of the kids he went to school with. What's more, he had other, more important things to think about, things like taking a trip over to Sag Harbor to see what he could find out about the headless yachtsman, as Basil had called him. He grinned. Basil was a pretty funny guy.

Through the shrubbery that screened the deck from the road he watched a brown van glide slowly past. He waited till it was out of sight, then walked down to the wall by the road and tucked himself in against the stones where he lay hidden by the barberry bushes at the end of the wall. When they came back, they couldn't see him and he'd be able to pick off their license plate number.

Only a short way past the house the road ended in a small turnaround and it didn't take the van long to reappear, again traveling slowly. He heard the engine just on the other side of the wall and then the back of the van came into view. New York plates? A chimney cleaner from New York here in Madison? It so took him by surprise that Max nearly forgot to read the license plate.

Not until the van had rolled safely out of sight down the narrow road did he climb out from under the bushes and brush himself off. Then he walked inside, wrote down the number, picked up the phone, and called Uncle Carl.

"Hi, Mrs. Field, Max Murphy, is Uncle Carl there?"

"Max, I know you're trying to help with this, but you simply can't keep calling here. Right at this moment your uncle is talking to some federal people."

In the background he could hear Uncle Carl shouting at someone and he grinned. Uncle Carl was not big on federal agents.

"As soon as he throws them out, could you have him give me a call? Just remember, Mrs. Field, *omnibus est parabulum*."

"What?"

"It's Latin."

"I knew that," she said, falling into the trap. "Oh, you might as well wait," she said. "They're leaving now."

A second later Uncle Carl sighed into the phone. "What's up, Max?"

"There's been a brown van cruising slowly past the house. I took down the license plate." He read it off. "I thought the New York plates might be important."

"Good work, Max. I'll check it out."

"Uncle Carl?"

"Yeah?"

"You ought go easier on those federal guys, they might turn you in to the IRS."

Carl chuckled. "Stay out of trouble, Max. I already heard that you quit the soccer team."

"I signed up with Uncle John."

"You're playing for Guilford?"

"At least I'll be playing."

"Max, stay out of any more trouble, okay?"

"Sure."

No sooner had he hung up the phone than he was thinking about Meg's boyfriend, and this time it wouldn't go away. He was still thinking about him hours later when he rang the bell at the house.

"Hi." Meg opened the door. "Glad you could come."

"Thanks for asking me," he said. She was barefoot and wearing shorts and a polo shirt. Okay, first crisis past. Just one more to go and this was by far the nastiest.

"Everybody's out on the porch."

He walked alongside her into the enormous open living room, its windows facing the Sound, determined not to let anything change him. "Did Basil tell you about our conspiracy to rule the soccer league?"

She laughed. "It didn't sound nearly so grand when he said it."

"Ah, but it is, it is. Nothing like it since the Revolution."

They stepped onto the porch. "Max," Meg said, "this is Deidre Adams, my roommate at school. Deidre, meet Mad Max Murphy."

A girl! Her friend was a girl! And not just any girl, but a sleek chunk of perfection like Meg. "Hi," Max said, hoping his relief didn't show too clearly.

"Hi," she said. "From the stories I've just heard, you live a pretty exciting life."

Max grinned, the imp inside showing clearly in the twinkle of his eyes. "A body in motion tends to stay in motion until overcome by friction," he said, "or to quote Stephen Potter, 'but not in the south' because in the heat everything sweats and that provides enough lubrication to overcome the friction."

"What?" Deidre laughed.

"I told you," Meg said.

"Soda's in the cooler," Basil said.

Max reached in and pulled out a Coke. "Wanna take a boat ride tomorrow?"

"Where to?"

"Sag Harbor."

"What's in Sag Harbor?"

"That's where the headless yachtsman came from."

"A little hugger mugger is it?"

"Never hug a mugger," Max said. "They carry social diseases. No, I'm serious here. We're talking body bugs and other terminal disorders."

Now, he had them all laughing and Max sat down in the chair opposite Meg and took a long swallow of Coke, making a note to never ever again let his imagination trample rational thought. He'd wasted the better part of an afternoon over nothing. Ah well, he thought. Not exactly nothing. You can't be jealous without there being a reason and clearly Meg was the reason. How had he not known that before?

"Do we all get to go?" Meg asked.

"Sure, why not?"

"Just where is this famous Sag Harbor?" Basil asked.

Max pointed out across the Sound. "Right about there. I planned to throw in some fishing gear and maybe we could try Plum Gut, see if there are any blues or stripers around. There usually are, this time of year."

"Fishing?" Meg asked.

"Sounds absolutely terrific," Basil said.

"I'll get some bait," Max said. "Bunkers and eels."

"Eels?" Deidre did not look happy. "Aren't they some kind of snake?"

"No, they're fish that look like snakes." Max grinned, deciding not to tell them they were dead when he got them. It was a sneaky way to disinvite the girls, but he hadn't wanted to exclude them. Better to let them decide for themselves.

"Maybe Deidre and I will work on our tans," Meg said.

Max shrugged. "We can do some skiing in the afternoon," he said.

"What about soccer practice?" Basil asked.

"Right. Forgot. After soccer practice."

"What time in the morning?" Basil asked.

"I'll be at your pier at seven."

"I'll be ready. Anything I should bring?"

"Seasick pills, maybe."

"I never get seasick," Basil said.

"*Alia scramulus bulatum*," Max said.

Basil laughed. "*Funiculae odeatus*," he said.

"You guys are so full of it," Meg said.

"*Omnia salar simpleticulum est*," Max said.

"*Et bidular aquarius*," Basil shot back and then they all collapsed in laughter. And when that quieted down, Basil said, "how odd is it that both of us should have happened onto the same ploy?"

"Pretty strange," Max said. He finished his Coke. "After dinner maybe we could all walk down to East Wharf. The night crawlers will be out by then."

"Night crawlers?" Deidre smiled. "More snakes. Is that all you talk about is snakes?"

"Different kind of worms," Max said. "Townies and beachies. A clash of the social classes. Territorial warfare resembling dog packs, a lot of profiling and strutting."

"Ah," Basil said, "the inevitable *strum und drang* of teenagery."

"Oh, God," Meg said as she groaned. "This is your fault, Max. You got him started, you encouraged him."

"Cool," Max said.

Ten

The Fur Starts To Fly

Dinner, Max decided, was excellent on all counts. The food was superb and Lord and Lady Greene were relaxed and, unlike most adults, they not only talked but listened, which was pretty much of a surprise after all he'd heard about the stuffy English. On the other hand, he held his "Max-talk" in check, switching to another brain channel which allowed him to tell stories, like the one about Mrs. Santorini. They especially liked his conversation with the guy in the BMW.

And after they had eaten he and Deidre joined in, carrying dishes to the kitchen, and then Lady Greene shooed the men out and they adjourned to the porch where Lord Greene lit a cigar to complement his Remy-Martin brandy.

"Tell me, Max," Lord Greene said, "what do you think these murders are all about?"

"You want me to guess, sir?"

"It strikes me, Max, that I have seldom met even an adult who dissembles so effortlessly or so well."

"I'm good at that," Max said as he grinned. "I can disassemble anything, but I'm really good at parsing outboard motors."

Lord Greene laughed. "No wonder you and Basil get along."

"Talking with Max is a lot like breaking code," Basil said. "You're never quite certain just what he's said."

Max grinned.

"But you still haven't answered my question," Lord Greene said.

"What do you know about Plum Island?" Max asked.

"I know what they do out there."

"I think it has something to do with Plum. The headless yachtsman, as Basil calls him, came from Sag Harbor. He was an environmentalist. But what's really weird is that, according to my Uncle Carl ..."

Basil interrupted. "He's the Chief of Police."

Lord Greene nodded. "Always good to know bloodlines and political connections."

"Uncle Carl says that the FBI, the CIA, and the DEA are all investigating this, along with the State Police. He threw a bunch of them out of his office this afternoon, but I don't know yet what that's all about, except that Uncle Carl doesn't like federal types."

Lord Greene drew on his cigar. "The CIA? Now that's odd. Under your laws they are enjoined from acting on domestic difficulties."

"So it must be international, then," Basil said.

"So it would seem," Lord Greene said. He sipped his brandy. "What a delicious mystery!"

"I'm putting my money on Uncle Carl," Max said. "He's solved some really tough cases. Most people think he's just a local cop, but he's really good at what he does. He's never been to college but he's read all the books they read and he's spent a lot of time talking to the state forensic guy about how to handle crime scenes and how to look for evidence."

They looked around as the girls joined them.

"Ready?" Meg asked.

"Where are you going?" Lord Greene asked.

"Just up to East Wharf. Mom said it was okay," Meg said.

Her father grinned. "What do you call it these days? Hanging out?"

"Dad ..." Meg groaned.

"Have a good time, but don't make it late."

And with that request tucked safely away they walked up to East Wharf, just a short way from the house.

The crowd had gathered, as they have on summer nights since anyone can remember, Max thought; teenagers, doing what teenagers do, getting together in groups to sneer at other groups. But they weren't part of any group and Meg and Deidre made things interesting. Even the guys who were paired off with summer dates turned and stared, which left their girls incensed over the invasion of such serious competition.

And then it got a lot more interesting when Watkins and a couple of his buddies from the football team showed up. If Watkins was big, the guys from the football team, Jack Snow and Angelo Agostinelli were even bigger ... like houses. Bullies. Ever since first grade they had been beating up on someone and they had always gotten away with it, mostly because everyone was afraid of them. Well, almost everyone, Max thought.

Basil saw them too and he leaned toward Max and in a

very low voice asked, "trouble?"

"Maybe," Max said. "No need for you to get into this, Basil."

"I've been in a scrap or two." Basil grinned.

"Those are football players," Max said. "They thrive on pain."

"I can supply plenty of that," Basil said.

"What is all this mumbling?" Meg asked.

"Nothing," Max said quickly.

They walked toward the beach and a bunch of kids gathered at the edge of the parking lot and Max took over. Maybe it was all the years in the restaurant, or perhaps it was simply his extroverted personality, but Max moved easily into the group. "Hey, guys," he said, "This is Basil Greene and his sister Meg and her friend Deidre." Then one by one he introduced the kids from town.

The thing about Max was that he had a special status among the rest of the kids. He wasn't the most popular guy in school, and he wasn't the best student, and he certainly wasn't a star jock (yet), but he was Mad Max Murphy, and when he showed up the fun started. So anybody that Max introduced found an open door, and it wasn't long before they were all talking and once the girls discovered that Meg and Deidre were only summer people, and therefore only a temporary threat in the matter of attracting the hot boys, they relaxed enough to suspend their cattiness, at least temporarily.

Watkins, Snow, and Agostinelli cruised the edges like predators waiting for the opportunity to spring. But it was tricky. The cops patrolled the beaches at night and there were plenty of adults around and these days everybody carried cell phones. And they did know who Max's uncle was, so that figured into the formula. They also discovered that Max always knew where they were, tracking them as if he came equipped with radar.

All of that added to their frustration and frustration breeds impatience. And when they finally tired of walking around with their shoulders bunched up like fighting bulls, they drifted toward the group. They didn't think it would be much of a challenge. Nobody was as big, and nobody they could see had a reputation for fighting. It was gonna be a walk in the park.

"Hey, Murphy," Watkins said. "You still think you're a tough guy?"

Max turned and looked right at him. "Nobody wants any trouble, Watkins."

"Who says," Agostinelli shot back at him, laughing. "Some of us like trouble."

"Com'on, Angelo, get off it." Max said. "You've been watching too many mob movies."

Agostinelli pointed with his great ham-like hand at Max. "You watch your mouth, Murphy. You're talking to an enforcer here."

Max raised his right had as if offering a benediction. "*Omnes Gallia in tres partes divisa est,*" he said.

"You really are a wise-ass, aren't you," Snow said. "I heard that about you, but I didn't know till now what a wise-ass you really are. You know what happens to guys with big mouths?" He stepped closer, his fists clenched.

"I wouldn't do that," Basil said quietly.

"Who are you?" Snow asked.

"A dream you'll wish you never had," Basil said.

"An Englishman? One of them sissy Englishmen?"

"This is ridiculous," Max said. "You guys have any idea

how ridiculous this is? You come here looking for a fight and no matter how it turns out, everybody loses. What do you think happens when your coach finds out you've been bullying up on people? What if somebody reports you to the cops? What then? You go to court for assault, you get off with a slap on the hand, but you won't be able to play football. Have you thought about that?"

"You can't hide behind your uncle forever, Murphy," Watkins said.

"And you can't hide behind these overdeveloped gibbons," Max said.

"What does that mean? What's a gibbon?" Snow asked.

"Forget about it," Max said.

"No. We ain't gonna forget about nothing! I think youse're giving me a load of crap here and I don't take no crap offa nobody," Agostinelli said

"Max," Basil said. "Is this chap speaking English?"

"The hotter they get, they more they sound like actors in a B-grade film," Max said.

Agostinelli rushed him, hurling a wild overhand right and Max stepped to the side and let him fly past, then whirled and kicked him in the crotch from behind as hard as he could, sending him to the ground collapsed in a symphony of groans that only comes from a guy who's been whacked in his hanging down parts.

Snow charged at Basil, leading with his head, like the football player he was. Bad mistake. Basil hit him in the face four times, concentrating on his big pulpy nose where you can hit someone without damaging your hands, and then when Snow straightened up, Basil stepped in, his hands like light sabers as he concentrated on Jack's exposed midsection.

It happened so fast nobody had a chance to move except those who were already in motion and Max was in motion, closing on Watkins, and dropping low he came up at him, his right hand burying itself in Preston's solar plexus. He grunted once and sagged, dropping to the ground almost in slow motion to join his buddies.

Max stepped back. "You didn't tell me you were a boxer," he said to Basil.

"It's those sissy English public schools."

Max grinned, then looked around as Sean pulled his cruiser into the parking lot, climbed out, and walked toward them. Even in the growing summer dark you could see his smile.

"Whoa, what have we here? Looks a lot like a fight." He shone his flashlight onto Watkins, Snow, and Agostinelli. "You have anything to do with this, Max?" He shook his head. "Naw, thin guy like you. No way you beat up three guys this big. It looks to me like the three biggest bullies in town got into a fight with each other. You never know, do you?" He switched off his light. "Guess I'll have to talk to their parents and their coaches and warn them about this stuff. Can't have fighting, you know. It's against the law. Disturbing the peace." He looked down at the would-be assailants. "As soon as you can get up, I think you guys better get on home. Probably the rest of you ought to get along as well."

The kids, still wide-eyed, still agog over what they had seen, began drifting away and Max, Basil, Meg, and Deidre did the same.

"Nice bit of fun that was," Basil said. "A proper dust-up, if ever there was one."

"I don't believe you guys," Meg said. "That was ... awesome! Those guys were so much bigger!"

Diedre looked admiringly at Basil. "I never saw anything like that! I mean, you hear about fights, but you never see them. God, my heart is still pounding."

"Adrenaline," Max said. "The wonder drug that nobody can outlaw."

"You're a nasty guy in a fight," Basil said. "Where'd you learn to fight like that?"

Max shrugged. "I have this thing," he said, "if I see somebody do something once then I can do it. Sometimes I can just make it up. I see myself doing it and then I do it."

"Now that is out there," Meg said.

He thought at first it might be a criticism, but when he looked at her he saw something else and he hoped it was not his busy imagination putting in more overtime, because he thought there was a glimmer, a light in her eyes that might mean more, and Max liked that idea a whole lot.

Eleven
Across To Sag Harbor

Basil stepped down into the boat and they headed out into the Sound. The morning was clear, with a soft southwest breeze and Max pushed the throttles up to cruise and took a bearing on Orient Point, just visible on the horizon.

The deep-V hull of the boat devoured the low swells, and the Honda engines ran quietly, allowing them to talk in only slightly raised voices.

"I thought we'd hit Sag first and then fish on the way back. That okay with you?" Max asked.

"Sure."

He wanted to ask about Meg, but he couldn't for the life of him think how to get it started without seeming too eager. Basil helped him out.

"You certainly got my sister's attention last night."

Max grinned. "She's a really great girl," he said.

"As sisters go, I've done pretty well."

"You never know how girls are gonna react after they see you in a fight."

"Actually, I think she's quite taken with you."

That was about the best news he'd heard in a long time, Max thought. "She is very cool, Basil."

"You should tell her that."

The idea was almost beyond comprehension.

"Well, I think she knows already, but it can't hurt to say something."

"I don't know. I mean, well ..."

He laughed. "You won't have to come up with a pedigree, if that's what you're thinking. The parents are well removed from the older generation."

"Well, it isn't like we were getting married," Max said.

"A little soon for that, I should think. Of course there's no accounting for you Yanks."

Max grinned. "I promise you'll be the first to know."

Basil looked at him, then laughed.

"How's your hand?" Max asked.

"A bit stiff. I caught his cheekbone."

"I'd like to learn how to box," Max said. "That was an awesome display."

"Be glad to give you some pointers, though it might be like carrying coal to Newcastle. I never saw anyone move so quickly as you did when you sidestepped Angelo."

"I thought of myself as a matador," Max said.

"First bullfighter to ever kick the bull in his privates, I'll wager." Max turned the bow into the swells left by a passing yacht. "Who was that cop? I meant to ask you last night, but I forgot in all the excitement."

"Sean and my brother have been best friends since anyone can remember."

"This place is more ingrown than a Welsh village!" Basil laughed.

"It's a long story but the short of it is that those guys have been bullies for a long time and nobody minded that we kicked their butts. And they can't do anything about it because once Sean talks to their coaches, those guys will have to stay squeaky clean or they won't play."

As they talked they neared the halfway point and suddenly what had been just a string of low lying lumps on the horizon became the shore of Long Island stretching both east and west nearly out of sight.

Without warning Max pulled back on the throttle and the boat slowed to a crawl as he lifted the butts of the casting rods from the tubes by the gunwales.

"I thought we were fishing on the way back."

Max pointed off toward Six Mile Reef. "Birds," he said. "Gulls. That means there's blues working. You never pass up an opportunity." Holding the rod, he cut the wheel, shifted to forward, and then increased the speed slowly as they came up to where the birds were sitting in the water snapping up the pieces of small fish that rose to the surface. Some lifted up and dove into the water.

"Okay," Max said. "You'll fish from up forward. Cast out toward the birds and let the lure settle. Count to ten and then reel a short way, then let it settle again. Sometimes it helps to jig the lure."

"Show me what you mean," Basil said, "I've never done this before."

Max idled the engines, shifted to neutral and let the boat drift on the tide. The chop was heavy here but nothing the boat couldn't handle. He fired the lure out toward the birds and turned the handle on the big spinning reel to reset the bail and a second later a blue smashed into the lure and Max set the hook.

"They're here!" Max shouted. "And they're taking. Get forward and have at it!"

Basil stepped quickly to the open front of the boat and unleashed a cast. The lure fell maybe eight feet before a blue hit and he set the hook. "Bloody hell!" he shouted. "This is a huge fish!"

As blues go, they weren't monsters, but they were substantial fish in the eight to ten pound class and on light tackle it's hard to find a fish that fights harder. They run, they sound, and sometimes they even burst through the surface in wild leaps. Both of these fish stayed down but it still took thirty minutes to land them.

Max netted his first, and, trapping the fish in the mesh of the net, he used a pliers to take out the hook before dropping the fish into the well in the back of the boat.

"Walk back this way, Basil," he called. "It's easier to net them."

Basil, his attention focused on the fish, edged toward the stern and then swung the rod toward the boat and led the fish to the net.

"What a bloody fight!" Basil said. "My arms are falling off!"

"You did a great job." He picked up the pliers.

"Why do you need a pliers?" Basil asked.

"Teeth," Max said. "Lots of razor sharp teeth." He dropped the fish into the well and looked up. The school was still there but now they were surfacing and he quickly jointed up two fly rods and handed one to Basil.

"Now, this is the sort of rod I understand," Basil said.

"I'm gonna move up closer. As soon as you can reach the area where they're coming up, start casting."

He eased the boat forward, the engines only running

hard enough to maintain way. He was seventy feet away when Basil started his cast and it was clear that he had done a lot of flycasting. His form was perfect and he generated a huge amount of power when he shot the rod forward, the line snapping through the guides. The fly hit the water and a fish hit the fly and the fight was on.

Max idled the engines and let the boat drift as he shook out some line and began casting. He picked a spot, aimed, and once he had enough line in the air he let it go. The fly dropped just where he had wanted and he twitched it once and a big blue took it hard.

Blues are fun no matter how you catch them, but on a fly rod everything is bigger and it takes a good deal more skill to land them. But on this day, the blues were over matched. Basil had cut his teeth on Atlantic Salmon in the Spey in Scotland and Max had been catching blues since he was old enough to hold a rod.

When they finally boated the fish, the school had gone and the gulls had begun to move away. They stowed the rods and Max got his bearings and headed off toward Long Island.

"My God, that was fun." Basil said. "How much do those fish weigh?"

"Around ten pounds."

"Well, that was a lot more fight than I ever got from a salmon, even a big salmon." He clapped his hands together. "This is turning out to be the best summer ever."

"Next, I'll have to take you striper fishing. The Sound is a great fishery."

"And they're all good cating?"

"The best. You like sushi?"

"Absolutely."

"Stripers make great sushi. Dad just hired a Japanese chef to run a sushi bar. It starts this week, I think."

"You'll never keep my father away now. He is absolutely addicted to sushi." He grinned. "You know, at the end of the summer we're going back to England for two weeks. Think you'd like to come along?"

"You're serious?"

"Of course."

"Then round up the usual suspects!"

"I'll take you salmon fishing. We have our own beat on the Spey. You'll have a smashing time. Maybe we'll even get you up on a horse."

As they approached Orient Point they ran in the lee of the land where it cut off the southwest wind and then came around the point into the wild rip that is Plum Gut and finally headed up the bay to Sag Harbor running across the wind. Max pulled into the dock and tied up by the gas pumps. Then they climbed out and walked up to the small building at the end of the pier.

Del Woodcock sat behind the counter reading his newspaper. He looked up and lowered the paper. "What can I do for you?" he asked.

"Need gas and ice," Max said.

"Got plenty of both." He smoothed his gray hair and stood up and he was a lot taller than he had looked while sitting.

"Might's well get the ice on the way out. How much you need?"

"Have you got it crushed?"

"I have."

"Four bags."

He took a ring of keys from his pocket, opened the machine, and pulled out four bags of crushed ice. "Been fishing?" he asked.

"There was a school at Six Mile," Max said.

They walked out on the pier to the boat and Max climbed down and took the bags of ice from Basil. Then he opened the fish well, opened the bags, and poured the ice over the fish.

"What are they? Ten pounds?"

"That's my guess," Max said.

"How bad was the rip out there?"

"Average," Max said as he opened the fill cap on the gas tank, took the hose from Mr. Woodcock, and began filling the tank.

"See you're from Madison," the old man said. "You hear about our Mr. Waterstreet?"

"I was sitting on the beach when the boat came ashore," Max said. "Pretty nasty."

"You saw him then?"

"I was the first one on the boat."

The old man shook his head. "Terrible thing."

"Did you know him?" Max asked.

The man pointed to a forty-foot boat tied up by a pier a short way down the harbor. It was rigged for commercial fishing. "That's his boat, or I should say his company's boat."

Max looked up. He was sure he'd seen rattier looking boats, but he couldn't think when. But what caught his eye was the big red bull's eye on the stern. "What's the bull's eye for? Make sure somebody sinks it on the first shot?"

Mr. Woodcock laughed. "She may look like a derelict, but that's only on the outside. I spent a lot of hours working on that boat and she's as ship shape as any boat you'll ever see. Put a monster of a Cummins turbo diesel in her just this past winter and she's got every navigational device known to man."

"I didn't know he was a fisherman," Max said.

"He wasn't. His company does environmental work."

"What kind of work?"

"Snooping mostly," the old man grinned. "Word around here was he'd been trying to find out just what was going on out on Plum. Fella told me he had a big contract with one of them tree hugging groups, but I wouldn't put much stock in that. Oh, he was into something unusual all right, no mistake about it, but my guess is he was a smuggler."

"Why would you think that?" Max asked.

"Came and went in the dark. Always in the dark."

"Drugs?"

"Nope. Something else. DEA people watch this harbor round the clock. They searched him a couple of times but all they found was plankton samples, all put up neat in jars."

"Then what makes you think he was a smuggler?"

"You sit here on this pier long enough, watching boats coming and going, you get a sense of how things are."

Max shut off the gas and handed the hose back up to him. Then he reached into his pocket, took out his wallet, and handed up a credit card.

"Well, if not drugs, what was he smuggling?"

Del finished filling out the credit card slip and handed it down to Max to sign. He pointed back to the building. "I live right there, upstairs, and I'm a terrible light sleeper. Three times this past month a big brown van was waiting for them when they pulled in. Each time they took some crates off the boat and loaded them into the van. Dead of night it was. Not much happening, that time of night. Even the cops are asleep."

Max handed him the slip and the man looked at the signature and handed the card and the receipt back. "There could be lots of explanations," he said.

"That's what I said, but then he suddenly turns up murdered and that changed everything, don't you know."

"Has the boat gone out since?" Basil asked.

The old man raised his eyebrows at Basil's accent. "You come a long way just to fish," he said.

"My family lives here now," Basil said.

The old man nodded, but he had suddenly grown suspicious. "You going back out fishing?"

"Probably try the Gut and maybe the Race," Max said. "But right now I was hoping we could tie up and go get some breakfast."

He hesitated, rubbing his chin. "I suppose," he said. "How long you gonna be?"

"An hour," Max said. "Gotta stay on the tide."

He pointed to the end of the right hand arm of the T-shaped pier. "Bring her up inside down there. But no more than an hour or I'll have to charge you."

"Fair enough," Max said. "And thanks. If I had to wait much longer to eat, my stomach would start digesting itself. Sometimes I think I'm part gull."

The old man smiled at that, but Basil's accent had clearly thrown him out of trim.

Max decided to plow right in. "Something we said?"

The old man shook his head. "Wasn't what was said, but how it was said." He looked at Basil. "One of the fellas worked with Mr. Waterstreet had an accent just like yours, and suddenly I thought maybe I was talking out of school."

Max laughed. "Not likely. We're just kids, you know. It was pure coincidence I happened to be on the beach."

"Now that I think of it, you look sort of familiar."

"I'm Max Murphy."

"Tom Murphy's boy?"

"I am."

He smiled and the lines in his face relaxed. "Thought your boat looked familiar."

"Has Waterstreet's boat been out recently?" Max asked again.

"Last night, as a matter of fact. But the van never showed up."

Max started the engines. "What about Mr. Waterstreet's family? They must be pretty upset."

"Never saw 'em. I heard they live in the midwest somewhere. Rumor was, he'd been divorced a long time." He untied the bow line and handed it down to Basil. "Keep it to an hour," he said. "Things get pretty busy this time of day."

"Yes, sir. And thanks."

"Say hello to your father. Tell him Del Woodcock says hello."

"I'll tell him," Max said and then dropped the engines into gear and motored off down along the pier.

Basil waited until they were out of earshot. "Came a cropper on that one," he said.

"Did you get the feeling he doesn't like the guy with the English accent?" Max asked.

"Could hardly have been clearer," Basil said.

They tied up the boat and walked back to the building, turning left and heading up into the village.

"Where are we going?" Basil asked.

Max gestured with his head. "To the building with the red bull's eye."

112

"You're going to just walk right in?"

"I don't know yet. First I have to see what it looks like."

Basil grinned. "You're more fun than a barrel full of eels."

The streets were crowded with summer people awash in tinny, harsh New York accents, so rich in the know-it-all tone of voice that they might as well have been walking down Fifth Avenue.

"There's an awful lot of people," Basil said.

"Let's get a cup of coffee and sit over there and just watch for awhile. See if anyone comes or goes from the building."

They stopped at a coffee shop, and Basil surprised him by buying a local newspaper, which he tucked under his arm as they carried their coffees a short way down the street and sat on a bench along the sidewalk.

"This place sure has changed," Max said. "It just gets slicker looking every year."

"Pretty smarmy all right," Basil said and then he opened the paper and began reading the front page while Max sipped at his coffee and watched the people and kept an eye on the building. There was what looked like an office in one corner but there were no lights on inside. Waiting also gave him time to consider whether this was such a good idea. Clearly, it wasn't something you wanted to lose your head over. He grinned at the turn of phrase.

"Anything interesting in the paper?"

"There's a story about Waterstreet. I would gather he was quite well known. This wouldn't seem to be his main office, either. They used this for storage of equipment for the boat. They did a lot of marine surveys for people wanting to put in piers and bulkheads and jetties. But I would gather that business wasn't all that good because of the trouble getting anything approved by the Army Corps of Engineers." He sipped his coffee. "Who are they?"

"Government men. They have final approval of any project near the shore or harbors. Very nasty. They're on us all the time about the decks and piers at The Trap, but they can't do anything. We're grandfathered. Two years ago Dad filed suit for harassment and then got our Congressman to tell them to back off. Even with that, not a month goes by that they don't send an inspector out looking for some technicality."

"Sound like a fun-loving bunch."

"I don't think there's anyone inside the building," Max said. "Let's finish our coffee and then try the door."

"Just walk right up and try the door?"

Max grinned. "Sure."

Basil smiled back at him. "You certainly know how to show a guy a good time."

Twelve
Steady Bearing ... Decreasing Range

Max tried the door handle and then knocked, but no one answered. He looked round at Basil, grinned, and walked down the street and then turned into an alleyway. Halfway down, the building jutted inward where the land gave way. Supported by stout pilings, the rest of the building jutted out over the water to a pier which wrapped the weathered gray structure back to where they stood. A set of stairs ran up to a door from the pier.

They could only be seen from the water and just now the harbor was quiet and the only boats they could see drifted quietly on their moorings.

Max, with Basil just behind, climbed the stairs and Max walked to the door and turned the handle.

"Did you think it would be open?" Basil asked.

"Worth a try."

"Okay, what next."

"We try the basement. Most old buildings like this had a trap door in the floor where they shoveled out the remains after they got through processing the fish."

They had to wade, bent over to keep from hitting their heads, and in the middle row of pilings Max found what he was looking for. The trap door was damp and the wood looked old and half-rotten but when he pushed against it the door was solid.

"Is it locked?" Basil asked.

"I don't think so. Most likely swollen shut. Give me a hand."

Basil slipped in next to him and now they pushed upward together and the door began to give. On the second push it gave again and stopped.

"Once more, I think," Basil said.

"Okay, on three. One, two, three!"

They used every bit of strength they had and the trap popped free, the hinges squealing as it opened into the dark of the building. Max climbed in and then Basil followed. At first the dark inside seemed so dense they had to depend on what little light came from the trap. Then slowly their eyes began to adjust and they discovered that the walls had thousands of cracks where the boards had pulled apart over the years and after several minutes they could see quite well.

"What are we looking for?" Basil asked.

"I don't know," Max said. "Some kind of crates that fit into a van."

"Let's split up and ..."

"No," Max said. "Stay together. That splitting up stuff is for the movies. Two of us can see and hear more and we can warn each other."

There was little to see. The big open room was empty and not until they crossed the rails once used to haul fish from the pier was there the least sign of anything having happened there in twenty years, except that the rails were shiny and well oiled. They followed them toward the front of the building where the rails disappeared behind a wide door that was solidly locked. Max scratched his head as he looked around for another entrance.

"Where do you suppose that ladder goes?" Basil asked.

"Let's give it a try."

Max went first, climbing the ladder to a broad landing that ran all the way to the front of the building. Off to the side they found another trap door, this one leading to a flight of stairs. Down they went, feeling their way along the walls in the dark, expecting another blind alley, but this time the door was not locked and they eased it open and stepped into a room lit by a row of small windows up near the ceiling.

A battered wooden desk stuck out from one wall and a wooden chair had been shoved into the kneehole. Three metal folding chairs stood by the desk. Against the back wall they saw a mound of what looked like long boxes covered by a tarpaulin.

"All right!" Max said softly.

They rolled back the tarp to reveal three long crates, nailed solidly shut.

"Is that Russian?" Max asked as he pointed to the writing stenciled on the lids.

"It most certainly is." Basil took a deep breath. "Max, I'm getting sort of a bad feeling here. I think we may be in rather too deep."

"Yeah, I'm thinking the same thing."

Outside they heard a vehicle pull up, stop, and then back toward the double doors that opened into the street.

It was already too late to escape and there was no place to hide, save one. The doors started to open and they flipped the tarp back over the crates and took the only option available. They crept quickly around to the back of the pile, crawled under the tarp and lay close up against the boxes.

They heard the vehicle back into the building and then the doors closed and the vehicle backed closer, stopping a few feet away.

"Okay," a raspy voice called out and they heard the engine shut down and the footsteps of several men.

"How many are we getting?" a man with a much higher-pitched voice asked.

"Just one. The rest we get later." His accent was decidedly English, but unlike Basil's it was harsh and rough.

"I think we oughta take 'em all now," another man said.

"The van won't take but one at a time," the Englishman said. "The boss said just one."

"Somebody's gonna come looking."

"We'll store one and then head right back. Maybe we'll come back with the other van too."

Another man spoke up. "I want to know who the hell killed Waterstreet? It don't make no sense."

"Who cares? Maybe he didn't pay his bills. Anyway, all he did was bring stuff in."

"So who brings stuff in now?" Tony asked. "This here was good steady work."

"There's plenty of guys with boats, Tony."

Max held his breath as he felt the tarp move. "Tony, grab the other end of the tarp," the Englishman said.

They flipped the tarp upward, folding it back only just enough to expose the uppermost crate.

"How long are we gonna be on the payroll?" Tony asked.

He sounded, Max thought, like some of the guys he had heard in New Haven.

"Who knows. You never know with jobs like this." He laughed, "Hey, is the money good? You're damn right it's good. So just forget about it and get to work."

Several men grabbed hold of the crate and with a huge grunt hoisted it away. Max and Basil heard it slide over the metal floor of the van. The doors clanged shut, two men pulled the tarp back into place, climbed into the van, and then, as the van began to pull on out of the building, Max peeked out from under the tarp. It was a brown van but the license plate was different. The doors to the building closed and he heard the lock snap shut. Slowly they crawled out from under the tarp, looked around to make sure they were alone, and when they saw no one, they took one look at each other, turned, and fled back up the stairs and across the loft and down the ladder and then through the trap and into the water.

Quickly, they waded out from under the pier and then up the alleyway and into the street. As they passed the front of the building they looked toward the double doors. They were closed and hanging from the hasp was a big brass padlock snapped closed.

Once past the building they broke into a run, heading for the pier and their boat. Soccer players can run, even goalies can run, and within less than a minute they were underway and headed out of the harbor.

"Now, that was bloody close!" Basil said as he caught his breath. "Too bloody close."

"We're lucky we heard the van pulling in or they'd have caught us red-handed. What I want to know is what was in those crates."

"Missiles," Basil said.

"Missiles! How do you know that?"

"I speak and read Russian."

Max reached for the cell phone. "Steer the boat. I gotta talk to Uncle Carl."

"Hello, Mrs. Field, it's Max."

"He's busy, Max."

"Whatever he's doing, it doesn't matter."

"He is talking with the first selectman."

"This is an emergency."

"Max, with you, it's always an emergency. You'll simply have to call back and that's all there is to it!"

' "Mrs. Field! There's no time to argue!"

"Max, are you on a cell phone?"

"Yes."

"Well, I can hardly hear you. Why don't you go find a regular phone and call back."

"I'm on the water just outside of Sag Harbor and there's not a phone booth in sight."

"Well, you'll still have to call back."

He heard a voice in the background and then a man came on the line. "Who's this?"

"Max Murphy, who are you?"

"This is Sergeant Grub. Now what is this all about. And make it quick. You're tying up a line here."

"I need to talk to Uncle Carl."

"The Chief? You need to talk to the Chief?"

"Right. Uncle Carl. Please put him on."

" This phone is for police business only."

"This is police business."

"Of course it is. Kids call here all the time on police business. What do you take me for, a fool?"

"Hey, it's your choice, Sergeant. You want me to take you for a fool, I'd be glad to. But in the meantime, if you like working there, put me through to Uncle Carl."

The phone went dead. "Damn! He hung up on me. That miserable, over-bloated, doughnut-eating maggot hung up on me!"

"Why can't they just take us seriously?" Basil asked.

Max punched in the number. "Mrs. Field, you tell that giant worm that the next time he hangs up on me I'm coming down there and cut off his pant legs! And if you hang up on me I'll cut yours off too!"

"You know what you need, Max Murphy, is a good hiding. You just wait till you uncle hears about this! In fact, I'm going to get him right now."

Max grinned. More than one way to skin an adult, he thought, and then he heard Uncle Carl shouting. "You did what? You hung up on him? You miserable excuse for a cop, don't you ever hang up on him again!"

And then another voice came up in the background. "Carl, you can't talk to Edgar that way. It's not professional."

"George, let me tell you something. I've had about enough of your nepotism and on Tuesday I'm laying it all out for the Police Commission. You made me hire him and he isn't qualified to do anything but make the morning doughnut run! So here's the deal. He's fired. Turn in your badge and gun, Grub. You're done as of this minute! Now if you'll excuse me I've got a call to take."

"You can't fire me!" Grub shouted. "I'm a sergeant. You can't just fire a sergeant. He can't do that, can he George? Tell him, George."

"You can't fire him without just cause."

"He works for me and I can fire him. You got a problem

with that check with the town attorney. I already did. Now get out of here. I got a police force to run!"

He could hear a lot of scrambling in the background and then the sounds of someone crying.

"Max," Uncle Carl said. "What's up?"

"I was just in a warehouse in Sag Harbor and we found some big crates with Russian writing on them. Basil Greene, who was with me, says they're Russian missiles. He can read Russian. And they loaded one of the missiles into a brown van and drove off. It's a brown van like the one I told you about but the license is different." He recited the numbers and letters from the plate.

"Son of a … Max, where are you now?"

"We're just heading into Plum Gut."

"What else can you tell me?"

"There's two more missiles left in the warehouse and they're expecting another shipment and they mentioned Waterstreet too."

"Did they see you?"

"No. We were out of sight."

"You're sure."

"Positive."

"Did you talk to anyone else?"

"Just the guy at the gas dock."

"Del Woodcock. Great. Got a mouth bigger than a grouper. Look, you get back here as fast as you can. I don't know what's going on, but you can bet somebody was watching that warehouse. Probably the guys in the van don't even know about the place being watched. You just crank up your engines and get home!"

"Okay, Uncle Carl."

"One more thing. Do you understand now why I told

you not to get into this?"

"No more investigating. I promise."

"Get going."

He switched off the phone and slipped it into his pocket. "As one defenseman said to the other, time to get the puck out of here!" He pushed the throttles to full and the boat shot forward, skimming along the bay at almost forty-five knots.

"What's going on?" Basil asked over the engine noise.

"Uncle Carl says to get home fast. He says there was probably someone else watching the warehouse. Someone the other guys didn't even know about. If they saw us we could be in deep do-do. You watch back aft for anything that looks like it's following us."

"Bloody hell, this is exciting! My God, what a boring life I've led."

"Just hope they don't have a really fast boat," Max said. He took a bearing with the compass and then held a straight course running on a long diagonal. The wind had come up some and now the boat flew through the chop, seeming to leap from each wave and throwing a great wash of water to the sides as the bow came down against the sea.

But it was an illusion because the stern never left the surface and the engines hurled them along. "Keep a sharp lookout." Max said. "They could come from anywhere."

They were well inside Six Mile Reef and driving for home when Basil tapped him on the shoulder. "There's a boat coming from our right. I can't say for sure if it's headed for us, but it's going very fast."

Max looked quickly to his right, gauged the speed of the boat as best he could, and then checked their own speed and made a quick calculation in his head based on when they were likely to reach the same point on the water. It was a rough guess at best. The only way you could really work it out was by using the radar to get the speed and then plotting the courses on a chart. But the way it looked, they should come together just on the other side of Tuxis Island, and at that point he had an advantage because he knew the waters.

"Is he trying to intercept us?"

He switched on the radar. "Take the wheel."

Basil slipped into the pilot's seat and Max pulled out a chart laminated in plastic. He checked the radar screen, marked the bearing and speed and then with a ruler and a felt marker he drew a line. Then he checked their speed and bearing and drew a second line. Close. He'd been very close, off by no more than a hundred yards. They'd be nearer to West Wharf when they met. "His speed is steady and his bearing is steady and it looks like he's picked a point for intercept. Steady bearing and decreasing range mean collision. But it could be nothing. It could just be somebody running along the shore." As he looked again the bearing changed and the intercept point shifted seaward. The boat was going almost sixty miles an hour!

"Shift your course five degrees right," Max said.

"Five degrees right rudder, aye," Basil said and it was clear that he was thoroughly enjoying this madcap dash.

Max unlocked the compartment on the right side and pulled out a stainless steel shotgun. He loaded in five rounds, pumped one into the chamber, and put on the safety.

"Damn! You've got a gun!"

"You never know, when you're on the water."

"Is that legal?"

"Sort of. I've got a hunting license, but it's a junior license. I'm supposed to have an adult with me." He slipped the gun into a holder in the console, which kept it ready but out of sight. "I guess I'll worry about that later." He checked the boat on the radar, and as he had suspected, they'd come around five degrees and that put them even closer to intercept.

"Can we go any faster?" Basil asked.

"No. But we can go a little slower." Max backed off on the throttles the least little bit. "Let's see how good these guys are and whether they're really after us. "

"What are you trying to do?"

"Make him second guess us. Okay, come back to the original course and give it full throttle." He watched the other boat closely on the radar, timing it with his watch, waiting for them to change course again, but ten minutes later they had not. They were aimed out to sea and they'd cross their wake well behind unless they changed soon. But the boat ran steadily and for a second Max began to breathe easier. No. I know what he's gonna do, Max thought, he's gonna run right up our wake! And he's got the speed to catch us.

"Ten degrees right rudder," Max said and Basil brought the boat onto the new course. They'd cross closer together now, but he'd have to turn to pick them up. And then suddenly the other boat corrected course toward shore and Max ran the calculations again. He grinned. Now, on the low tide, the rocks at Madison Reef were only just under the surface. He could tilt his engines up and they'd glide right over them, while the bigger boat with its inboard engines would not. It'd take the bottom right out of the boat at that speed.

"I'm seeing that grin," Basil said.

"Better let me take the wheel," Max said. "This is gonna get real tricky." He slid into the pilot's seat and slipped the bow shoreward and this time the other boat turned with them and a minute later ran into the rip off Meig's Point. It slowed them considerably and that was what Max needed to lead the way down along the shore.

"I think they're gaining," Basil said.

"Let me know if they change course."

"Aye, matey."

Max shook his head. Either Basil didn't understand the danger or he was one very cool dude under pressure. But then he'd been totally under control last night too, so it must be the latter. No wonder the guy was all-prep.

It seemed to take forever before he spotted the rip at Madison Reef and now he picked up his landmarks and pointed the bow dead at Hogshead Point.

"They're gaining fast," Basil said. "You want me to man the shotgun?"

"Can you use one?"

"I've been shooting since I was seven."

The boat started into the reef and Max shot for the big swirl in the current, setting his hand on the switch and then counting slowly, hoping he had got it right. He clicked the switch and raised the motors and the boat slowed and then Max lowered the engines and the boat shot forward. He had figured they'd come right up his wake to take advantage of the flat water he left behind, but he had not in the least anticipated what would happen.

The bottom of the boat caught the rocks and when the fuel tanks ruptured the whole boat leaped upward out of the water a good ten feet, rising on a huge yellow and red fireball and two limp human figures shot upward and fell back into the water. Max dropped the speed to idle and brought the boat about. Pieces of wreckage coated with fuel burned as they floated on the surface.

"Wow! Smashing! Absolutely smashing! I had no idea what you were doing! Damn, Max, you are a genius!"

Max dug out his cell phone and dialed the number. "Hello Mrs. Field," he said, "can I speak to Uncle Carl?"

"Certainly, Max," she said and he wondered what Uncle Carl had said to her. Must have been unpleasant at best.

"Max! We just got a report about an explosion out at Madison Reef and I'm guessing it wasn't you."

"It was the guys chasing us. I led 'em onto the rocks."

"Can you see them?"

"There's two of them, both floating face down."

"Unload the shotgun and stow it."

"How'd you ..."

"Let's just say I made an educated guess."

"Whoa, good call," Max said.

"Is there any sign of life?"

"None that I can see."

"The harbor patrol is on the way and the phones are going nuts! You get out of there now before somebody gets close enough to identify you. I don't want any reporters picking up on this."

"We're as good as gone," Max said. He switched off the phone, put the helm over, and jacked the engines up to full throttle.

"What's up?" Basil asked.

"Unload the shotgun and stow it. Uncle Carl told us to blow out of here and that's what we're doing."

Thirteen

A Surprising Discovery

Max sat at the round oak table while both his father and mother paced around the kitchen circling like hungry sharks.

"You've really done it this time," his father said. "I mean you've really done it. I can't believe what you've done." He stopped and looked down at Max. "Have you got any idea how dangerous that was?"

His mother stopped and looked down at him. "My God, Max, you could have been killed!"

Max looked up. "Have you ever thought of putting a pickle and onion sandwich on the menu in the bar. I mean, you could use those big Vidalia onions and gherkins and lots of mayo and ..."

"Max!" his mother shouted. "This is serious!"

"Do you know what happened when the police stopped the van?" his father asked. "Those guys came out shooting! One officer was wounded and two of the men in the van were killed! Max, for God's sake, Max!"

He sighed. "Okay, I was wrong, but I had no idea it would lead to something like that. We were just nosing around and all of a sudden we were right in the middle of it." He wondered how Basil was making out. Probably not much better. "And then when we were coming home some other guys came after us."

"I don't think I believe this," his mother said. "How could you do that?"

"I used the radar and charts. And I kept changing course and speed to make them guess wrong so they'd come up behind us, so they had to come up our wake, and ..." He grinned. "I'm sorry, okay. I got into something I didn't even know was there."

"Crap!" his father shouted. "Absolute crap! Two people get beheaded and you didn't think there was any danger? You must think your old man is a pretty dim bulb, huh, Max?"

It galled him. It was like a fire in his brain. He knew he was wrong but they wanted him to admit he was wrong and he wasn't about to admit that. Not now, not ever! Or was it that? Wasn't their anger a reaction to the danger he'd been in? What would it be like to have your kid nearly get killed? He guessed maybe that was something you couldn't really measure until you were a parent, but it had to be nasty, very nasty.

"Well at least you're safe," his mother said.

"I really am sorry," Max said. "One thing just kind of led to another."

"Why did you go to Sag at all?" his mother asked.

He rattled off a string of little lies. "We were going over to fish the Gut and the Race and I was down to a half a tank of gas, so I decided to go into Sag to fill up. And then we got talking to the guy who runs the marina." He shrugged. "What do you want me to say? That I was stupid? Okay. I did something dumb." He couldn't believe that he'd admitted that. But then he didn't believe the way he'd lied either.

His father stopped and poured a cup of coffee. "It was just damn lucky they ran onto the reef."

"It wasn't luck," Max said. "In fact, in a way, it was your fault."

"My fault?"

"You made me memorize all the charts. All I had to do was get them to follow my wake and then I lifted the engines just before I came to the rocks and we went right over and then I lowered the engines and they came down our wake like they were in a tunnel."

His father nodded. "That was smart, Max. That was really smart. And you said before that you used the radar?"

"They were trying to intercept us. But once I figured out the timing, I kept altering course and speed and threatening to cut in behind them and they decided there must be an advantage to coming in behind, so they changed course. And they didn't know about the rip off Mcig's and that slowed them down and gave me enough time to set them up."

"Tom, is that possible? Could he have done that?"

He nodded. "He could have. And in fact, look at what happened. Those two guys in the boat were literally blown apart with the boat." He looked at Max. "I don't suppose you remembered the shotgun."

"Loaded and ready and Basil's been hunting since he was seven and I'm gonna guess here, but based on his ability as an athlete, he wouldn't have missed."

Suddenly the atmosphere in the kitchen had changed. His parents were quiet, watching him, and shaking their heads, and he had no idea what that meant because it was a set of signals he'd never seen before. "Am I gonna get grounded?"

"No," his father said. "No, Max, that wouldn't do much of anything. All we're asking is that you stay out of this; that you have nothing to do with it. Play soccer, work on your hydrogen project, hang out with your friends, and stay out of this thing. It isn't over. Carl tells me that there are more officials into this than he's ever seen. It's big time, Max, and it leads to some very powerful people. You already know how ruthless they are."

"Uncle Carl said somebody must have been watching the warehouse. That's how they identified us. We could still be in danger."

"I hadn't thought of that," his mother said.

"I think they'll be a little too busy to worry about revenge," his father said. "Oh, yes. One other thing. It seems there was a fight last night at East Wharf ..."

"You talked to Sean?"

"He couldn't wait to tell us how you and Basil took out two of the biggest, toughest guys in town." He shook his head. "How the hell did you manage that?"

"Basil knows how to box and those guys are kinda slow."

"Max, could we spend the rest of the summer just being bored?" his mother asked.

Max grinned. "*Fundulatum, pabulatum est.*"

"Max ..."

Clearly this wasn't going to fly. "Okay, okay, but I still think a pickle and onion sandwich would be a big hit."

Max spent the rest of the day working on his project,

wondering the whole time whether Basil had gotten into trouble and why there was no answer when he called.

By six o'clock he stood back and looked at his hydrogen generator and decided it was ready for a test run, except that he didn't have enough sunlight to really give it a good test. And anyway, he was hungry. He walked to the house, expecting to smell something cooking, but no one was home. Instead, there was a note.

"Max," it read. "You'll have to eat at The Trap tonight. Sorry, but I had to help out."

He dropped the note on the counter, walked outside, and climbed onto his bike. No big deal. It might even be fun. He could take his dinner out onto the private deck out back and watch the sun go down.

At Greenhill Road, he slowed for the traffic and then pulled out and pumped up to speed, cruising along in the shade of the trees and finally breaking out into the sunlight. He saw a red BMW pull out of a driveway up ahead and immediately he thought of Mrs. Santorini and the red Beemer … and then he remembered the pin the guy had worn. His system went to full alert. Had the guy been waiting for him? How could he? How could he have known I'd be riding my bike here? He was letting his imagination do the driving and that was not good. After all, there were a lot of red Beemers around.

Max held his speed, watching the Beemer pull away and disappear around a turn in the road. As it left him behind it seemed to drag the images that had been digging at him all day into the open. He could still see the bodies of the two men flying through the air and then lying face down in the water. There was no escaping the fact that he'd killed them, and no matter what anyone said, no matter how much he had been justified, it did little to off-set the fact that he had killed them. You couldn't just ignore something like that. He wondered if you could ever really got over it, and then he decided that probably you could. Soldiers did. Cops did. At least as far as he knew, they did.

He rounded the corner just before the turnpike overpass and then put his head down, stood up, and drove the bike hard, pumping up the shallow grade. From there on, it was downhill to Route 1 and The Trap, but he kept his speed up, working his leg muscles, and that helped to shove at least some thoughts farther back into his mind.

Better still, when he looked out into the dining room, there were Basil and Meg and their parents. He couldn't decide whether he ought to say hello. After all, he had put their son in considerable danger and he doubted any parent would appreciate that. He walked back into the kitchen and watched his father cut him a big slice of prime rib. He loaded on some French fries and some salad and then got a Coke and walked back out onto the deck.

Wayne was sitting there eating his dinner. He grinned. "So, little brother, I hear you went big time."

Max sat down at the round table. "What's that supposed to mean?"

"Relax, will you?"

"I don't like being criticized."

"It was a compliment, Max. Chill, man."

"Sorry," He cut a chunk of meat and stuffed it into his mouth.

"Dad told me all about how you used the radar and charts." He shook his head. "The whole town is talking about it. You ought to go into the bar."

Max shook his head. "I could have got Basil killed," he said. "I should have stayed out of it like Uncle Carl told me to."

"Maybe, but I also heard him tell Dad that if you hadn't gone prowling around they'd never have found those missiles."

"I still shouldn't have done it."

Wayne shrugged. "Well, if it's any consolation, big guy, there isn't anyone in town who isn't a little jealous. First you hammer those knuckle heads and then you eliminate some bad guys, some very bad guys. And you do all of that in twenty-four hours. That's pretty incredible, Max, even for the Madman."

He grinned back at his brother. "Sometimes I wonder how I get into this stuff. I mean, why me? Why am I the one who always seems to be there when stuff happens? It's pretty weird, Wayne."

Wayne shrugged, pushed his plate away, and pulled the big puffy chef's hat down over his thick black hair. "Well, look at it from my point of view. The closest I've ever been to anything strange happening is when they toss some drunk into the creek."

Suddenly they heard a lot of shouting up by the bar and then a great splash and the lifeguard scrambled into the rowboat. They laughed as they watched the drunk sputtering and waving his arms, treading water as he drifted on the incoming tide. His language was largely unprintable but then that's why he'd gotten thrown overboard.

The skiff closed on him and he reached up and grabbed onto the gunwale as a bunch of guys up by the bar started singing: "What shall we do with the drunken sailor, what shall we do with the drunken sailor, what shall we do with the drunken sailor, er-liee in the morning?"

That was followed by another splash and then Pete, the lifeguard looked up and shouted. "Hey! I only got one boat here you know! Let me get one ashore first from now on, okay?"

"Who are those guys?" Max asked.

"There's a bachelor party. Pete's gonna be busy."

"Maybe we ought to just throw a net across the river," Max said.

"Seine 'em up like sardines." Wayne stood up. "Oh well, back to work." He grinned. "And thanks for suggesting those pickle and onion sandwiches. I never sliced so many onions in my life."

"They like them, huh?"

"They love them! What made you think of that?"

Max shrugged. "Every time I look into the bar it looks like a pickle and onion crowd."

"Talking to you is like talking to someone from another planet. Just what does a pickle and onion crowd look like?"

"I don't know. I just know when I see one."

"Well, let me know when you spot one that'll go for capers. I ordered way too many capers."

"I'll keep my eyes peeled," Max said.

Wayne laughed and walked back toward the kitchen and Max went back to eating the best prime rib known to man. Four or five bites later, he heard someone come out onto the deck but he didn't turn until Basil sat down at the table.

"So, matey, what's next?" Basil asked.

Max grinned. "You okay with your parents?"

"It was a bit dicey at first, but I think that in as much as I survived they're not too terribly upset."

"They must be pretty mad at me, huh?"

"Strange, that. I'd have guessed they wouldn't allow me to see you again, but my father was so impressed by the way you used the radar and your knowledge of the water, that it seemed to override everything else."

"And your mother?"

"She'll probably have something to say about taking foolish risks."

Max nodded. "How did you know where I was?"

"I saw you when I went to the men's room. We're having dinner here."

"What about Meg?"

Basil grinned. "Do I detect a growing attraction toward my very attractive sister?"

"I told you before. She's a great girl, and I never said that about any girl before. Yeah, I like her."

"Well, unless I miss my guess, the feeling is mutual."

Max smiled. "Really?"

"She literally hung on every word when I told them what happened, and I'm guessing it wasn't her brother she wanted information about."

"Whoa, that's cool. That is definitely cool."

"You want to talk to her? I'll go send her out."

Max felt a surge of panic. What would he say? He'd be here alone with her and … and he didn't know whether he could handle that. He grinned. "Sure," he said.

Basil smiled and clapped him on the shoulder. "You are one tough guy, Murphy. I didn't for a second think you'd go for that. I wouldn't have."

There was a sudden rash of shouting from up by the bar and then a great splash and they heard Pete curse and shove the boat out into the creek. "I hate bachelor parties," he said loudly enough for everyone to hear.

"Are you sure you want to do this?" Basil asked.

"Yeah. I can do this. I mean, why should it be so hard? And if things don't go okay, I'll just jump into the creek."

Basil laughed. "I'll get her."

He'd finished his roast beef by the time she came out and sat down across from him.

"Hi," she said.

"Hi." He smiled and she smiled back.

"You guys nearly did it this morning, huh?"

"Pretty close," Max said. "I think we found out how curious cats wind up."

"How do you like Deidre?"

"She's very nice."

"We get along really well, and that's more than I can say for most roommates. Generally, they fight like alley cats."

"I think Basil likes her quite a bit."

"Hmmm, that's what I thought too. But what I wanted to know is how much you like her."

He grinned, the imps dancing in his eyes. "I like you a lot better," he said.

At first he thought she was gonna run off like a startled deer. "Are you always so blunt?"

"Yup."

She laughed now and then she reached out and put her hand on his arm. "I like you too, Max."

For what seemed a very long while they said nothing. They just looked at each other, thoughts racing, trying to make sense out of what no one has ever made sense of in all of history.

And then suddenly she blushed. "I have to get back. Will you be coming down tonight?"

"Are you sure it's okay?"

"I'm sure. We can all play a board game or something."

"What time?"

"We'll be back by nine at the latest."

"Thanks. I'll be there."

She smiled and then turned and walked away and he watched her until she disappeared into the dining room. Slowly he shook his head. Go figure … his heart was racing faster now than it had with those guys running that big boat up his wake. There was nothing to do but see where it led, and that was okay with him. Out of the corner of his eye he saw his mother step away from the screen door to the kitchen and he felt as if someone had just dumped a pail of ice water over his head. It was as if he'd been caught doing something he wasn't supposed to. What sense did that make? None. And it didn't matter whether it made any sense or not because he liked Meg and she liked him and there was nothing more to consider. It was turning out to be one heck of a summer.

More shouting and then another splash and Pete scrambled into the boat. He left his plate on the table and walked down the steps to the lower deck which was in real-ity a pier that ran along the creek. "Hey, Pete," he called. "You need a hand?"

"Thanks, Max. I can use all the help I can get." He hadn't reached the first guy when there was another splash and Max grabbed the long pole and ran to the end of the pier. Hand-over-hand he ran the pole out into the creek and the second guy caught hold of it and Max pulled him in to the ladder. The guy was laughing so hard he could hardly climb up onto the pier.

"I never had so much fun!" he shouted as he crawled

up onto the decking, got to his feet, and headed back for the bar. "Thanks," he called over his shoulder and then disappeared inside.

Max shrugged. It was a warm summer night and the floor in the bar could take anything. He took a deep breath and let it out slowly. All he had left to think about this summer was Meg, soccer, and his generator.

Pete pulled on the oars and when he hit the pier, Max extended his hand and pulled the wet guy up onto the pier.

"Best party I ever went to," he said. "Awesome! Totally, absolutely awesome!"

Pete threw a clove hitch around the piling to secure the boat. "Thanks," he said and then he poked him in the ribs. "Hey, who was the babe you were talking to?"

Max grinned and said nothing.

Fourteen
The First Game

They played their first game away on Sunday afternoon against Old Saybrook and by any measure it was a rag-tag ugly affair ... at least for Guilford. With the best players in town off at soccer camp, they had only some freshmen and some beachies who at most played for jayvee teams.

There were some guys who might make the grade in the future, but they weren't there yet and, worse, as is so often the case with younger players who have been poorly coached, they were all trying to be stars. Once they got the ball, they wouldn't give it up, but tried instead to dribble all the way to the goal. The most any one of them made was five yards before an Old Saybrook player tackled them and took the ball away.

That meant Max had a very busy afternoon, which suited him just fine. After all, the worst part of playing in goal was the inactivity. You could wait all game long for one chance to make a tough stop, and you spent most of the time adjusting your defense, fielding a lot of slow rollers, and putting the ball back in play where your teammates had a chance to start a run upfield. In that attitude lay the basic difference between the goalie and the rest of the team. His job was to stop people from scoring and theirs was to score. His job was to anticipate what was coming and make the right moves to stop it. To do that you had to stay alert to any player over midfield. You had to know where they were and you had to wait and counter their moves without committing yourself until the play broke. The guys on offense were the bullets in the gun.

The first few stops were routine, just coming out to take away the angle on the shot and then deflecting it one way or the other. Sometimes he only had to smother the ball and then kick it downfield. And Max Murphy could kick it a long, long way. What's more he was accurate and the third time he fielded a ball at the top of the box, he saw Basil take off down the sideline, angling toward the middle of the field. He picked a spot well ahead of Basil, and whaled his foot into the ball, giving it everything he had.

The sheer length of the kick caught the defense flat-footed and the ball squirted past them and there was Basil, cutting in behind them, following the ball, easily onsides, as he pushed the ball ahead at a dead run, completely behind the defense and with only the goalie to beat. It wasn't even a contest, and when the goalie came out, knowing that was his only chance, he got an up-close-and-personal look at why Basil was all-prep. He seemed to carry the ball on the top of his foot as he spun at the last second, the move carrying him past the goalie and into the open and then he rifled a low screamer of a shot into the far right corner and they were up one to nothing.

But what happens once in soccer, a play that works, a

pass just right, is almost impossible to repeat because there are simply too many variables. Then, too, the opposing players adjust and now when Max fielded the ball, the defense moved back to keep him from getting a kick past them and the other players swarmed at him.

Max knew what they needed, Basil knew what they needed, and Uncle John knew what they needed, but the other kids on the field were clueless. Another ball rolled toward him with nothing on it and this time as he scooped it up, Max took his time, watching Basil talking to their center, telling him where to go and what to do.

Maybe it was the way Basil told him, or maybe it was the fact that on this field, or maybe on any field, he was the big dog, but whichever, the kid did what he was told, faking a circle back to start the ball up field and then slipping into a spot on the field about ten yards ahead of the defensemen.

Max kicked it right at him, bringing the ball up short so the kid took it on a single hop off his chest, turned, and chipped the ball over the defense, and there was Basil, once again following the ball perfectly, talking the pass before the defense had a chance to turn, and the goalie knew he was cooked. He did everything he could, but one-on-one, Basil was not stoppable, and when the goalie tried to come out and flatten out the shooting angles, Basil simply spun past him again and lobbed the ball into the open goal. It was a work of art, a symphony of athletic skill.

At halftime, Uncle John, who had once been the king of shoreline soccer players, and later an All-American at Southern, talked about passing. That's all he talked about and he said he didn't care whether they even got close to the goal as long as they got their heads up and began to see the field and their teammates.

"This is a team sport. You can't play it any other way," Uncle John said. "The two goals we scored came from playing as a team." He kept his voice low and he didn't sound the least bit angry, but no one doubted that if they didn't do as they were told, they'd be sitting on the bench. "Each time we get the ball back, get to your position, look for your teammates. Never mind scoring a goal. Think about making a clean pass and then going to where you can get clear to take a return pass. One good pass and then another good pass. I don't want anyone dumping it in and chasing it. We'll pass our way in. And don't forget who you're looking for. Know where Basil is at all times. Look for him. Lead him. The idea here is to win and assists count almost as much as goals because without assists there are no goals."

And once the game started again, Basil was all over them like hot sweat. It began to work, but in having to concentrate so hard on passing, the defense began to fall apart and ten minutes into the half, two Old Saybrook players got behind the defense and made a run at the goal. What saved Max was that they were overeager, both of them wanting desperately to score, and they failed to make the one extra pass that would have opened the goal. Even so, it was a tough shot to stop and for most goalies maybe even impossible. But Max knew from the way the kid flicked his eyes to the right and then angled his body to shoot left that the ball was going right and he took two quick steps to his left. The kid saw it and he knew the opening was gone and he tried to adjust to shoot left, but in making the transition he sacrificed his power and produced only a weak shot that Max dove for and deflected out toward the corner.

By then Basil had gotten back and when the Old Saybrook wing fielded the ball, Basil simply tackled him cleanly and rolled up onto his feet, getting to the ball just as another Saybrook player closed on it. Basil stepped to his left, flicked the ball left with his right instep, and when the guy went for it, Basil slipped the ball past him and ran the sideline.

Not even Basil could run fast enough to dribble faster than another player can run, but he managed to get to midfield before they closed up the defense. Instead of trying to get past them, he spun the ball back onto the front of his foot, tossed it in the air and with his back to the opposition he scissored the ball forward over their heads, fell onto his back into a roll, and came up running. The kid who'd taken the pass before had seen it coming and it would have worked perfectly if his timing had been right, but he'd been too eager and he'd gotten behind the defense before the ball. Offsides, and it went the other way.

The rest of the game was mostly just a lot of sweat and grunting with Basil directing the offense and Max setting up his defensemen, telling them which way to go, and who to mark, and it would have ended two to nothing if Basil hadn't gotten a penalty kick just outside the box. No contest. He simply drilled it, keeping the ball low, inches above the ground so it seemed to gain speed in the air. The ball was into the net before the goalie moved.

As he trotted off the field, Max realized that he'd been so focused on the game than he hadn't even noticed who was watching, and he was surprised when Wayne dropped down out of the bleachers and walked over to him.

"Hey, little brother," he said, "You were absolutely awesome! All this time and I never knew. I thought, you know, it was just a lot of talk."

All praise is good, but when it comes from your older

brother ... well nothing quite matches that, not even the good things your parents say.

"Max," Meg said as she walked up to them, "Max, that was great, I mean, really great. Basil said you were good, but I thought he was just exaggerating because you're mates."

All he could do was grin and then he remembered his manners. "Meg, this is my brother Wayne, Wayne this is Meg."

"Hi," she said and stuck out her hand, something girls never seemed to do. It was one of the things he liked so much about her.

She smiled as they shook hands. "It's nice to meet you," she said. "My father says you and your father can match any chef in Europe and believe me, coming from Father that is an enormous compliment."

Max grinned around at his brother. He was absolutely tongue-tied. The best he could manage was a thank you and a broad smile.

"Are you coming over later?" Meg asked as she turned toward Max.

"Sure. Just gotta shower up."

"Your brother is some kind of player," Wayne said.

"Oh, I know. He's almost too good. It makes him unbearable sometimes," she said, but you could tell that she liked having him as a brother. "Nice to have met you," she said to Wayne.

"Same here," Wayne said.

"See you later," she said to Max, offering a smile that would have melted the iceberg before the Titanic got there.

"Whoa," Wayne said as they both stood watching her walk away. "I didn't even know girls came in models like that. How old is she?"

"Fourteen. She just turned fourteen."

He looked around at Max and then back at Meg as she caught up with her parents. "You sure you're up to this?"

"No."

Wayne stared at his younger brother for several seconds, then looked back at Meg and shook his head. "I don't think any guy would be." He looked up at his little brother.

"What are you looking at?"

"All this time I've thought of you as my little brother, you know some kid who never did anything right. A little wise-ass who was always getting into strange kinds of trouble." He grinned. "I may have to change my opinion."

"Don't be too hasty," Max said. "I've got a lot of screw-ups left in me."

Fifteen
Mrs. Santorini Strikes

With his hair still wet from the shower, Max hopped onto his bike and headed for Meg's. The day had grown more humid and he could almost smell a thunderstorm coming on as he peddled at full speed toward the center, and then, on a whim, cut over to take the street that went between the school and Mrs. Santorini's house.

He hadn't expected to see her, but as he turned the corner two hundred yards away, there she was, dressed in gunfighter black complete with a black hat streaming rooster tail feathers. But she wasn't walking. She was hiding, waiting for a likely victim. Max pulled to the side, got off the bike, and concealed himself behind a tree, knowing she'd look his way once she started into the street.

She passed up two large SUVs and a Volkswagen Beetle and then came a powder blue Mercedes and she straightened up and started toward the street. What she didn't see was the police cruiser following the Mercedes. But her timing, as usual, was off by several seconds and the driver of the Mercedes was quick to his brakes, slamming them on as the ABS system took over and stopped him two feet shy of Mrs. Santorini.

The driver of the cruiser was not so lucky and he plowed into the back of the Mercedes with a loud crunch, sending it shooting forward. The car stopped with its bumper up against Mrs. Santorini's thighs. Max jumped onto his bike and raced down the street, as the cruiser door flew open and out popped Sgt. Grub. Now there's a surprise, Max said to himself, I thought Uncle Carl fired him.

Then the door of the Mercedes opened and Judge James Oliver Wilson raised himself up to his full six foot six inches. Max stopped across the street from them and sat on his bike seat, his arms folded across his chest.

At first Mrs. Santorini seemed taken aback by the sheer size and bearing of the judge. But it slowed her hardly at all. "Scalawag!" she shouted in her screechy, crackling voice. "You tried to run me down! Don't deny it!" She pointed at the judge with her cane as she closed on him.

The judge was in no mood to tolerate being shouted at, but he may have been oversensitive because he was a darker hue than most residents of the town (a point of some pride to those residents because he was one of the few African American jurists in the state). He was, however, famous for having a fairly thin skin in racial matters, and though he was a man well-known for his prodigious sense of humor, he was not a man to be trifled with either.

Grub suddenly hove to on the judge's starboard side. "You're under arrest!" he shouted.

"Certainly not!" the judge shouted back. "You rammed into me! You should be under arrest!"

Mrs. Santorini stepped around the Mercedes and stared at the two men, her cane raised, but it looked as if she couldn't decide who to whack first. That she would cane someone was never in doubt. Suddenly she nodded her head and whacked the judge in the back of his left knee.

"Ow!" he shouted as he bent forward and clutched at his leg. "Are you absolutely mad, Madam? You've just assaulted me!"

"I oughta assault you too," Grub shouted. "You can't go around just slamming on your brakes for no reason at all!"

The judge, caught between the two, much shorter assailants, looked as if he'd been set upon by a tag team of dwarves. He pulled himself up and squared his shoulders. "Do you know who I am?" he shouted.

"A sadist!" Mrs. Santorini shouted. "A sadist who gets his fun by running down old women! You saw him, officer! You saw him deliberately run me down!"

"All I saw was him lose control of his car and stop suddenly right in front of me."

"I stopped to avoid hitting this woman."

"No! You hit me!" Mrs. Santorini shouted. "Right here!" She pointed to her left leg. "I may never walk again!" she screeched, apparently unaware of how her statement conflicted with her behavior.

"Quiet!" Grub shouted. "I am the law here and I'm going to get to the bottom of this!"

It was a bad decision. Nobody told Mrs. Santorini to be quiet and she rose to the challenge as quickly as the grouchy guy who used to run the jewelry store. Fast as a fox she stepped around the judge and brought her cane down smack in the middle of Grub's hat, putting a considerable dent in the crown.

"Ouch, ouch, hey, you can't do that. I'm an officer of the law!" He took off his hat and felt his head and then, as he looked to see if there was any blood, she whacked him in the shins.

The judge laughed. "Hit him again! Smite him hip and thigh!"

Max grinned. It was a nice touch, getting the Bible into things. He pulled out his cell phone.

"Hi, Mrs. Field, just give Uncle Carl a message. Tell him I'm in front of Mrs. Santorini's house where she is beating up on Judge Wilson and Sergeant Grub."

"Max, this has got to stop! You can't be making prank calls to the police department!"

"I wouldn't delay on this one, Mrs. Field. Did I mention that Sergeant Grub managed to smash into the back of Judge Wilson's Mercedes? I think I forgot to mention that."

"My God ..."

"Maybe you better tell Uncle Carl to bring some riot gear. These people are pretty rowdy."

Quoting the Bible also seemed to have been a bad idea because Mrs. Santorini, a devout Catholic, whirled on him. "You sound like a Protestant!" The cane swooshed through the air and whacked him on the thigh. "There, take that! A little payback for Martin Luther!"

"Owwww," the judge howled. "Stop that! Stop that right now, you wizened old sack of ..."

"Don't get smart with me, young man! You young whip-persnappers think every old woman is a target for mayhem! Well, you got another think coming!"

"Madam, you are mad!" The judge shouted, but this time he leaped backward and escaped another whack.

Meanwhile, Grub had recovered and he grabbed Mrs.

Santorini from behind, pulled her arms around to her back, and slapped the cuffs on her. Somehow, she had managed to hang onto her cane and she snapped it sharply upward catching Grub squarely where guys don't like to get hit.

Now both of them were howling, Grub rolling around on the street in agony and Mrs. Santorini screaming something about rape and villainy as she struggled against the cuffs. Then the judge lost it, and when Grub's considerable backside presented itself he delivered a mighty kick.

That brought a strangely high-pitched wail out of Grub, and the judge, with a sadistic smile on his face decided one kick wasn't good enough and he leveled a second one straight at Grub's rump. Grub picked that instant to roll and the judge's foot went flying past, threw him out of balance, and sent him sprawling backward onto the asphalt with a great ripping sound as the seat of his pants gave way.

"Ohhh, my back. I think I broke my back."

Mrs. Santorini took one look and turned her head. "A flasher! The man's a flasher! What is this world coming too, handcuffing an old woman so she has to look at a flasher!" she shouted, as she took another look.

Just then a car coming the opposite way began to slow, the driver looking out the window. But she was apparently so horror-stuck by what she saw that she decided to end it all by driving her red Beemer smack into a large, unforgiving sugar maple just hard enough to burst the radiator and set off the air bag.

Max shook his head, wondering if this could possibly get any worse when Mrs. Santorini managed to get one hand free and with the cuffs dangling from her other hand she attacked the red Beemer, slamming her cane again and again onto the trunk of the car.

Maybe she's just got a thing about red Beemers, Max thought. In the distance and getting rapidly closer he could hear two sirens coming from opposite directions. One car was driven by Sean and the other by Uncle Carl. They pulled up and stopped and quickly climbed out of their cars.

Sean headed for the woman in the Beemer and Carl moved in and wrested the cane from Mrs. Santorini. "Anna, you've simply got to stop this," he said.

"Carl," Judge Wilson said, his eyes big and very round. "This woman is mad, mad as a hatter!"

Carl pulled out his handcuff keys and unlocked the cuffs. "Now, Anna," he said. "We're going inside. Katherine should be here any second now."

"He ran me down. The big one there. Absolutely flattened me!"

"Now, now, Anna I'm sure there's a perfectly logical explanation."

Max pulled a notebook from his backpack and began writing everything down in exact sequence. He read it back and then read it a second time. He signed and dated it and walked over to Sean, who had gotten the judge to sit in his car.

"Here's what happened," he said as he handed the paper to Sean. "It's all there right from the start. It was an ambush."

Sean laughed. "What?"

"Mrs. Santorini was hiding in the bushes, waiting for just the right car." He pointed to the paper. "It's all there."

Carl came back out of the house "How's the lady in the Beemer?" he asked Sean.

"She's okay. Just shook up."

Carl nodded. "I'll check on her again," he said.

In the distance Max heard another siren and he hoped the woman was all right. He thought she probably was because she hadn't been going all that fast.

Grub sat in the street, a large stream of liquid running from beneath him.

"Look at that," Max said, "I think Sgt. Grub should maybe start wearing some of those adult diapers."

Sean stared at Grub in disbelief, shook his head, and displayed a good knack for a pun. "I guess that ... Depends," he said.

Max laughed. "I've got an appointment," he said.

"You witness much more of this stuff, you're gonna wind up spending your summer in court," Sean said.

"How's the pay?"

"Terrible. You get nothing."

Max shrugged. "I've only got one route left between my house and the center of town where nothing's happened." He turned and looked at the judge. Never in his life had he thought of saying anything to a judge, let alone this judge, but whimsy carried the moment. "I saw it all, your Honor. All you did was stop in time to keep from hitting Mrs. Santorini."

The judge looked at him for several seconds and then smiled. "You've got to be Mad Max Murphy, right?"

"Yes, your Honor."

He pointed at Max. "Carl told me about what's going on. You follow his advice, you hear. Stay clear of this, Max. Stay as far away from it as you can get."

"Yes, sir." He swung his leg over the bike.

Sean winked at him. "Say hello for me."

"To who?"

"Miss Greene. Say hello for me."

"How do you know her?"

"My mother sold them their house. And she had me run through the mechanical stuff with them."

"And you've been talking to my brother."

"Of course."

"Jeesh, it's getting so a guy doesn't have any secrets."

"Who in Madison ever did?"

"The headless yachtsman," Max said. "And he's definitely not telling."

☞　　☞　　☞

He'd hardly pulled onto the road to the Beach Club when he picked up a red Beemer in his mirror. This one he recognized because the dents from Mrs. Santorini's cane still showed in the hood.

At first, until he remembered the bulls-eye pin, he thought it was just a freaky coincidence. But this was no coincidence. The guy had to be following him.

What did he want? Maybe it was because of the guys on the boat. Maybe he wanted revenge. Suddenly Max felt as if his stomach had gone solid and he could feel his legs beginning to shake. Not good. This was definitely not good. And the one thing he could not do was go to the Greenes'.

Okay, what then? Think, Max, think, he told himself. There's got to be a way out of this. He turned at the Beach Club and rode along the water. What he wanted to do was crank up and try to get far enough out of sight to make a turn or two and throw the guy off. But instead he slowed to a stop and waited, looking out at the water and watching the road out of the corner of his eye.

It didn't take long for the Beemer to show up and Max

took a long deep breath and made himself wait. The car came slowly along the road, staying within the speed limit and when it passed, the driver didn't turn his head. Max waited and after the car went round a bend in the road, he turned his bike and headed back the way he'd come.

When he stopped at the turn to West Wharf he spotted the car again, coming fast. Max turned right and then left as he headed for the Surf Club.

Unless the guy had a beach pass they wouldn't let him through the gate, and with New York plates there was a better than even chance that he wasn't local, although there were plenty of summer people from New York and they had passes.

He had almost reached the Surf Club when he turned and looked back. The Beemer was gone. All right! Maybe the guy hadn't been following him after all. Max turned the bike hard, guiding himself with his left foot against the ground, and then stopped and waited. Nothing. He waited several more minutes and still nothing. He started back the way he'd come, gliding along with the golf course on his left, and he was looking that way, when a man stepped out of the phragmities along the right hand side of the road and grabbed both Max and his bike.

"Hey, what the ..."

"Shut up and listen," the man said. He was tall and he wore chinos and a tee shirt and his arms looked like he'd stolen them from somebody in the National Football League. His black hair was cut short and when he talked his breath smelled of garlic. "We know you got it and it belongs to us. Give it to us and there won't be no trouble.

"What are you talking about. What have I got?"

"Don't play dumb. We got your number, kid. We know

how smart you are and we know you've got it. You saw what happened to the guy on the boat. Either give it back to us or we'll make sure you end up the same way. You got twenty-four hours." He handed him a piece of paper. "Follow these instructions. Exactly. No cops. No Uncle Carl. Nobody but you. No screw ups. If it's not there, then you can kiss good bye to your family." He let go and stepped back. "Get it done, kid. Get it done and everything's cool. Now get out of here!"

Max peddled as fast as he could, but instead of heading for Meg's he turned toward town and Mrs. Santorini's. Now he had to talk to Uncle Carl and that was all he could think about.

Sixteen
Shedding Some Light

When he reached the main road he stopped. He couldn't do it. He couldn't talk to Uncle Carl right now. He'd have to meet him somewhere in private. But where? For the first time in his life, Max Murphy did not know what to do or where to turn. He couldn't go near the Greenes'.

And then, out of nowhere, he thought of a solution. It'd be tricky and he wasn't even sure he could make it work, but at least it would give him a way to get past the deadline and then maybe he could figure out what it was they thought he had.

He rode for home, going over his plan as he peddled. It was probably crazy. He should just go to Uncle Carl and hope the police could protect them. Hadn't he always believed that? Why didn't he believe it now? How did you ever answer questions like that? With more questions? How else? He leaned his bike against the barn, walked inside and went to work. Two hours later he was still at it when his cell phone rang.

"Hello?"

"Max?"

"Hi, Mom."

"I thought you were coming down here for dinner."

"I got working in the barn and I lost track of time."

"Well, get on your bike and get down here."

"By the time I get down there and eat it'll be dark and I haven't got any lights on my bike."

"There isn't much in the fridge," his mother said.

"I'll make some spaghetti."

"How about I come up and get you?"

"That'd be great."

"Ten minutes. But be ready."

"I'll be ready."

It would have been best if he had been able to test it first, but there was no time for that. And then he remembered that it was Sunday night and Uncle Carl and Aunt Katherine would be there for dinner. He'd send a note to him with one of the waitresses and they could talk in the office.

He picked up the phone and dialed the Greenes'. "Hi, Lady Greene, it's Max."

"What a wonderful game you played today, Max."

"Thank you," he said. "But Basil was the star today."

"Don't be so modest, Max. I've seen a lot of footba … I mean soccer and Basil is absolutely right. You're simply the best."

Max grinned. "Thanks," he said.

"What I can't believe is that Basil tells me you're not going to play this fall."

"I want to, but the coach at the high school won't play

me, so there's no sense in going out."

"I'll bet the coach at Choate would let you play."

Now there was a different idea. Go to Choate? Turn into a preppie like all the summer kids? Whoa … "I wouldn't know about that. I mean I don't know how my folks would take it."

"You should think about it, Max. Then you and Basil could be on the same team for the next two years. Now, which of my offspring do you wish to speak to?"

"Well, both, but Meg first."

"Hang on."

"What happened to you this afternoon?" Meg asked. "I thought you said you were going to drop by."

She sounded pretty frosty, he thought. "I'm sorry," he said. "I was on my way and there was an accident and I had to stay because I was the only witness."

Silence and then a soft laugh. "How do you do that?"

"I wish I knew. I'm just there when things happen."

"Was anyone hurt?"

"No, but it was pretty strange. I'll tell you about it later."

"We're going to the movies tonight. Do you want to come?"

"I'd really like to," he said, hoping she understood from his tone how he wanted nothing more in the world than to sit next to her in a darkened theater. "But I can't. Something's come up and I have to take care of it."

"It sounds serious."

"It is."

"Are you all right?"

"Sure. Really, Meg, I'm okay. By tomorrow at this time it'll be all cleared up."

"It has something to do with the headless yachtsman,

doesn't it?"

"Something." How had she connected that?

"And you can't talk about it."

"Yeah."

"Max … is it dangerous?"

"No."

"It is, isn't it?"

Clearly, one word answers did not work with Meg. "Maybe, but I don't think so. It's more complicated than dangerous. It'll be okay."

"Max, you are scaring me here, and I don't like it."

"We can go skiing Tuesday morning," he said.

"Max … are you sure you're all right?"

He wasn't the least bit sure. He laughed. "I probably made it sound a lot more serious than it is. Honest, it'll be okay."

"Call me later, will you?"

"I promise. It might be late."

"That's all right. Did you want to talk to Basil?"

"Yes," he said, "just for a minute."

She laughed. "It's okay, Max. I promise I won't be jealous. I know you guys are great friends and I like that a lot. I'm the only girl I know who likes her brother."

Max laughed. "You two are something else."

"Hang on, I'll get him."

"Max," Basil said. "What in the devil is going on?"

"Meg will tell you. I just wanted to tell you that I can't make practice tomorrow."

"What?"

"Yeah, I know, I never miss practice, but something's come up. If I can get away sooner I'll be there, but I wanted to ask you to tell Uncle John."

"Sure. No problem."

"Thanks."

"You need some help?"

"Believe me, Basil, there's nothing I'd like better, but I can't get anyone else involved."

"What in the devil are you into?"

"You wanna know something weird? I'm not sure myself."

"Max, listen carefully. Anything you need, anything, you let me know."

"Okay. I can do that," he said, but they both knew he wouldn't ask. "I gotta go. Mom's picking me up and she just pulled in. I'll be at The Trap till ten if you want to get in touch with me."

"Max, watch yourself. We've got ten games left to play."

"It'll be cool."

☞   ☞   ☞

He ate in the office and when Uncle Carl arrived he sent a note out with the waitress. From behind the two-way mirror he could see the whole restaurant and he watched Uncle Carl and Aunt Katherine walk through the door to the back hall and disappear.

"What's up, Max?" Uncle Carl asked as he stepped into the office and closed the door.

"I need to know some stuff about the headless yachtsman."

Uncle Carl sat down. "What's going on?"

"I can't tell you. I wish I could, but I don't dare."

"Look, Max, you have to understand something here. I know you won't like it, but you are not an adult yet and

161

there's some things that kids can't do, because they can't always see what's coming. You learn that with experience."

He nodded, knowing that he had no choice but to share the risk. "I know why the guy on the yacht was killed. He had something that somebody wanted and he didn't give it up. They must have thought it was on the boat and they could find it, but they didn't. They think I found it because I was the first one on the boat and now they want it."

"Whoa …" Carl sat back in the chair. "And I'm betting that they've threatened to go after your family if you don't give it to 'em."

"Yeah."

"And you want to know what I know?"

"I need to know what it is they want."

Carl sat quietly, looking down at his hands. Slowly he raised his head and looked at Max. "This is top secret stuff. You can't breathe a word of it to anyone. I wouldn't even know about it if they hadn't needed my help. Someone on Plum Island apparently decided to sell some of the goodies they work with over there. This is nasty stuff, Max. It could kill a whole lot of people. In the right conditions it might wipe us all out. Up until now it was all guesswork. If Waterstreet hadn't lived in Sag Harbor nobody would have made any such connection. But because of that, the people there ran a few background checks and they turned up a big time gambler on their staff. Every weekend this guy takes the ferry to New London and goes up to Foxwoods. He mortgaged his house, everything he owned, and it still wasn't enough. So they think he decided to sell off some virus or bacteria to the highest bidder. Up till now they assumed he'd made the sale and Waterstreet was acting as the middleman to divert suspicion. They figured that

Waterstreet made the transfer and then they killed him, rather than paying him. They're gonna be pretty relieved to know that they've got a chance to get this stuff back because they have been acting on the belief that it had fallen into the hands of some pretty nasty people."

Max shook his head. "How bad is this stuff?"

"I told you. It could kill everyone on the planet."

"What would I be looking for?"

"Nobody's exactly sure."

"They must have some idea. How could they not?"

"All they'll say is that because of the security on the island, they're pretty sure it would be small."

"How small?"

Uncle Carl shrugged. "Maybe a couple of inches."

"What is it in?"

"Probably a metal vial of some kind, a test tube, but one that can be secured so nothing can escape."

"We need to go look at the boat again. Is it still there?"

"Last I knew."

"Let's go."

"Wait here. I have to talk to Katherine and your folks." He looked at his nephew very closely. "You okay?"

"I feel like I swallowed a live chicken."

Uncle Carl smiled. "Good. That's the way you should feel. That's the way I've felt ever since the federal guys gave in and told me what was going on."

☞ ☞ ☞

Uncle Carl stepped onto the boat, unlocked the cabin door, and stepped inside. He flashed his light around and when he found the switch, turned on the cabin lights.

"The feds went over this with a fine-toothed comb."

"Not fine enough, though. Otherwise they'd have found it." He stood in the middle of the cabin. Uncle Carl had turned his huge five-celled light on and was scanning the darker corners and then it clicked. Flashlight! He walked to the helm, reached out and felt under the rim near the window until his fingers closed on the small micro light. He unscrewed the end of the light where you loaded the batteries and dumped the contents into his hand. "Uncle Carl," he asked as he looked down at the silver tube. "Just how dangerous is this stuff?"

"I told you, Max." He followed the flashlight beam with his eyes.

"Would handling the tube be dangerous?"

"No. Only opening it."

"Well, maybe you should take a look at this."

He stepped over and looked into Max's hand.

"You think this is it?"

"Where was it?"

He held up the micro light. "Inside this. When we were here before, I saw this light and I have a thing about flashlights. If I pick one up, I turn it on. I thought the batteries were dead, so I set it back on the shelf and it rolled down into the drain well by the windshield. You couldn't see it. You had to know it was there."

"Put it back in the flashlight and we'll go inside the Coast Guard Station. We'll need a secure line."

Fifteen minutes later the vial was on its way back to Plum in a Coast Guard helicopter, and Max and Uncle Carl, after washing their hands in bleach, were on their way back to Madison.

"You've had quite a summer, here, Max."

"Weird. Even more weird than usual, which even for me, isn't normal. What's gonna happen to Mrs. Santorini?"

"We don't know yet. She might have to go into some kind of nursing home."

"Sounds kind of harsh. I mean, it isn't like she's sick or something."

"I know, but she can't go on running into the street all the time. Judge Wilson was pretty clear on that."

"Yeah, it was a bad idea attacking a judge."

"But some good came out of it. After the judge talked to our first selectman, I got to fire Grub again. Made my day, I can tell you."

They were almost to the Goose Lane exit in Guilford when Max spoke again. "We've still got a problem."

"I've been thinking about it. I'll call the FBI when we get back to The Trap and arrange a meeting. They'd like to catch these guys and maybe we can set a trap?"

"I already did," Max said.

"What?"

"I spent the afternoon in the barn. I'm pretty sure they were watching."

"So while you're gone they'll search the barn."

"Right."

"What will they find?"

"Something pretty nasty."

"How nasty?"

"I hope they're outside the barn when they open it."

"A bomb? Max, bombs are seriously against the law."

"So is killing people."

"What kind of bomb?"

"I don't even know if it'll work."

"Max. What kind of bomb?"

"Hydrogen."

"What!"

"Just the gas. It's in a piece of pipe."

"How does it detonate?"

"There's an electronic switch and a battery."

"What triggers it?"

"A remote control."

"What kind of remote?"

"Any kind of remote that uses a sonic signal."

They pulled into the parking lot at The Trap as Tom came rushing out. "I just got a call. My barn's on fire."

"Get in," Carl said.

Tom climbed in and Carl backed around, set the light on the dash, and turned on the siren as he stomped on the accelerator and tore out of the parking lot.

"Guess it worked," Max said.

"What else have you got in that barn?" Uncle Carl asked.

"Nothing explosive. There's some tanks with hydrogen in them, but they won't blow up."

"You're sure?"

"Max, what have you done?" his father asked.

"It's kind of a long story, Dad. I'll tell you later."

Uncle Carl picked up the microphone to his radio and called in to warn the firemen about the tanks.

"I told you, they won't blow up," Max said.

"We're gonna stay on the safe side with this, if it's okay with you, Max."

"Yeah sure. I just hope they put the fire out so I don't lose all my stuff. I spent a lot of money on that. At least the generator will be okay. It's way out on the lawn."

Carl made another call, this time to the FBI agent in charge and told him where to go. He hung up the mike.

"Now listen carefully. There will be no mention of bombs. This was a gas explosion."

"Bombs," Tom said. "You built a bomb?"

"Relax, Tom. Forget I ever said the word bomb. We even mention that and the ATF will be crawling all over the place like maggots and I don't like those guys. They're like somebody's private army, and they never get it right."

One look and they knew the barn was a goner. The flames had already eaten up through the roof and the fire company was working to contain the blaze by wetting down everything close by. The heat was so intense that it had blistered the paint on the red Beemer before the firemen had been able to drag it away.

The surprise was the guy lying on a stretcher.

"How badly is he hurt, Mary?" Carl asked the EMT.

"He's complaining of back pains," she said.

"How did it happen?"

"He's not saying much. We found him about ten feet from his car. He looks like he was standing there when something in the barn exploded."

"Did you find his car keys?" Max asked.

"That's why they had to drag the car away from the barn."

Carl frowned at him, and Max took the hint, but he knew what had happened. The guy had used a remote to lock his car and the signal had set off the bomb.

Carl took a pair of handcuffs from his belt, dropped onto one knee and handcuffed the guy to the stretcher.

"Whoa, what's that all about?" Mary asked.

"He's officially under arrest," Carl said, "and we absolutely do not want him getting away." He looked around, spotted Sean and called out to him.

"Yeah, Chief?"

"Watch this guy. No matter what happens you stay with him, understood?"

"Sure. Is he under arrest?"

"I cuffed him to the stretcher."

"What's the charge?"

"No charge yet. I'm waiting for the feds."

Sean's eyebrows elevated several notches.

"Is that the guy?" Carl asked Max.

"That's him."

"Carl," Tom asked, "what the hell is going on here?"

"Com'on," Carl said. "I'll tell you inside."

Seventeen
Not Just Another Match

Max stood in the goal, relaxed, working his fingers deeper into his gloves as he watched the game start. They were not the same team they'd been two weeks ago because now they had five Guilford varsity players, and Uncle John had turned out to be one heck of a coach. He had a particular knack for bringing guys together. They'd won all five of their matches. But so had Madison, because Jenks had rounded up ringers from everywhere, especially he had found guys to protect Preston. Even so, they'd allowed a lot of goals.

Nobody had scored on Max.

More to the point, when Madison and Guilford played against each other, there was a lot a stake. Bragging rights counted here because they were longtime rivals.

So for the first ten minutes, the game was played mostly near midfield. One lucky bounce changed that and suddenly Max had one guy on the wing with the ball and another coming fast behind the defenders and he knew what was next; a pass crossing toward the oncoming player. And as fast as he could run Basil wasn't going to get there in time to force the guy into hurrying. He had all the time he needed and the only chance Max had was to do what they didn't expect. So he waited until the guy on the wing started his leg into the ball and then he left the goal and ran for the spot where the ball and the player had to come together.

And Max could run. He could also growl like a bear, a big bear and the sound of his running and the deep rumbling growl put the player off his feed just enough to cause him to take his eye off the ball. And then Max leaped in front of him, slamming his forehead into the ball and snapping it back the way the guy had come. Todd Collins picked it up and fed a pass upfield.

As quickly as the ball had gone Madison's way it came back up the field on three incredibly accurate passes, the last from Basil, slipping it past the defense for Peter Parker coming in from the wing, and Basil faked his man and blew past, following Parker, shouting, "Behind! Behind you!" so Parker would know he was there.

Madison recovered quickly, but the reversal had happened too fast and Parker stopped at the box and let his shot fly. It was a bad shot, right at Preston, with no fake, just a straight flat shot. But instead of swallowing it up, Preston let it bounce off and Basil picked up the rebound, whipping the ball into the near corner.

It pumped them up enough to easily repulse the offensive charge that always follows a goal, and a minute later Basil shot one from the side, cutting it so the ball curved sharply. Preston dove, but he hadn't seen it coming, he hadn't seen Basil drive his left foot past the ball, imparting a sharp clockwise spin and the result was another goal.

The game got a lot nastier after that and it seemed like almost every play produced a yellow card. But Guilford had been ready for that and they refused to let themselves fall into the trap. Now, they concentrated on checking, on marking, on clearing, and they kept the game in the middle of the field. At the half the score was two to nothing.

They sat sprawled on the ground in the shade of a sugar maple as Uncle John stood in front of them. "That was a good half," he said. "We got to them early enough to throw off their game plan, but you can expect them to come out hard in the second half. We are not going to fall back and play defense. We are going on offense and we're going to take some risks here because we have a two goal lead and if we can get that to three, it'll take the wind out of their sails." He looked at Max. "It means the goalie will have more work. They're going to dump it in and follow it with everybody they've got. Our job is to reverse the flow, drive the ball our way. One more goal and then we play defense. Okay?" He nodded. "Rest up. It's gonna get busy and it's gonna get rough."

Max lay on his back looking up into the leaves, watching the way they half-swiveled in the light wind.

Basil sat with his back to the tree, his arms resting on his knees. "Sorry to hear about your barn."

"It was a nice old barn," Max said.

"You heard any more?"

"No. Nothing."

"The papers haven't said anything."

"Secret stuff. Everything about Plum Island is secret. Besides I don't think they've got all the people they want."

"That leaves you as bait, doesn't it?"

"That's why I can't come over."

"So what stops them from kidnapping you?"

"I've got more bodyguards than the president."

"Are you serious?"

"Uh-huh. Pretty much of a drag. Sometimes it feels like I'm hauling a barge behind me." He sat up. "The thing I don't like is not knowing more."

"It's the way governments work. It's even worse at home. And if you look at it from their perspective, you only ever tell anyone the least amount you have to."

"I just hope they know what they're doing."

"Why wouldn't they?"

"Because they didn't before and because we uncovered a missile running operation that was right under their noses, and they didn't even offer to cover my gas for the day. How cheap is that?"

"Maybe there will be a reward later."

"I doubt it." He slipped his hands beneath his head. "What's it like at Choate?"

"I like it, Meg likes it."

"Are you gonna go on boarding?"

"Once I get my license, then we'll commute."

"When do you get your license?"

"November. When do you get yours?"

"End of August."

"Are you interested in going?"

"Yeah, I think so. I mean, that way I get to play." He shook his head. "But my grades aren't very good."

"Like what?"

"B's. Do they have a test?"

Basil smiled. "I wouldn't worry about the grades. Our goalie graduated last spring and as far as I know we didn't recruit a replacement."

"So the grades won't count?"

"No, grades count, but they may not have to be as high."

"I could take a test if they wanted me to."

"You're really serious about this, aren't you?"

"I've been thinking about it."

Basil laughed. "I don't suppose Meg has anything to do with this."

Max grinned. "I've been thinking about that too."

"Oh?"

"I never met a girl like Meg. I never liked a girl as much as I like Meg. I'd like to see where it goes."

"Are you always so patient?"

"Always. Every time I ever get into trouble it's because I rush into something."

"All good things come to those who wait, my father says. I've always found it irritating. I hate waiting."

"It's not that I like waiting. It's just that when I wait, things seem to work out better. It doesn't mean I don't go crazy now and then. Sometimes you just can't wait. But mostly I'm pretty patient."

"How can you do that?"

"You know how. You do it on the field all the time. You bide your time, you wait for the play to come to you. I do the same thing in goal."

"And Meg? You can wait for Meg?"

"There's no choice. And anyway, I am what I am." He shrugged. "I can't change that. Right now Meg and I like each other a lot. But after you live in this town for a while you see things differently. People break up a lot here, especially in June so they can free themselves for summer. Then they get together again in the fall. It's crazy."

"How can you see things like that. I just play soccer and

tennis and I study. I want to get into a good university. I'd like to go to Yale. That sort of thing I can see clearly, but when it comes to girls, you can't predict anything. You can't tell what they're going to do next."

"I used to think I would pick a girl, but the way it seems to work is that they pick you." Max looked up into the tree. "It doesn't really matter. I mean, if you like her, what difference does it make?"

"None, I suppose, but it's a radical sort of concept."

Max grinned. "Probably wrong too, but right now it's keeping me out of trouble. Well, at least some trouble."

"Okay," Uncle John shouted, "let's get back out there."

They warmed up and from the instant Max stepped onto the field he was a goalie and nothing else. No other thought found room. Which is why when Madison made its first big push, he was able to make a diving save, deflecting the ball upward with the very tips of his fingers and then somersaulting onto his feet and leaping to the bottom edge of the crossbar and snatching the ball to his midsection.

He kicked it, a long flat kick just high enough to keep anyone from heading it until it began to drop, and Basil was on it, snapping a header to the wing and suddenly they had three men behind the defense and Preston never had a chance. He stood there, trying to decide which player to challenge, and by the time he went for the left wing it was too late. One pass and Basil had a wide open goal.

But now Madison had absolutely nothing to lose and they played like madmen. They took enormous risks and it worked. They got people free twice in the box and the first time Max exploded out of the goal and left the guy only one possible shot. It was a fake and the guy went for it as Max suddenly changed direction and blocked the shot with his body. The second time he had no chance. He simply had not expected the guy to shoot from so far out and he had focused on a second man coming in from the right.

By the time he recovered, the best he could do was get his fingers on the ball, redirecting the shot. He almost got away with it, and if the ball had been moving slower he would have. But the shot was bullet fast and it deflected off Max's fingers, hit the side of the goal post, and spun into the goal.

Max dug the ball out of the net, forcing his mind away from such an odious task. He hated having to retrieve the ball after he'd given up a goal. It was like having to admit defeat in front of everyone. It was like having to pick up a big dog turd. He threw it to the center of the field where it could become nothing but a ball again, but he marked the play in his mind. Never commit, he said to himself. You commit, you get burned.

The goal served to wake up his side and they played defense, marking their men so tightly that the balls that came toward him either were easily fielded or went over the endline. The match also got rough and play after play drew a yellow card from the ref.

Jenks ran up and down the sideline like a madman, shouting and waving his arms, appealing to his players to step up, to drive their play to a higher level. But Guilford just had too many guys who knew how to play and in the past two weeks at soccer camp, they had learned how to play defense. Basil was brilliant. He seemed to be everywhere, intercepting passes, tackling whoever had the ball, taking enormous risks, and succeeding at completely disrupting Madison's attempts to start any move to the goal.

Those who had come to see the match saw something

they had most likely not seen before; they saw that brilliance in soccer does not lie in scoring goals, but in the subtle midfield play that confuses the opposing team.

Basil was not alone. The other players caught the energy of his play and raised their game to yet another plateau. Suddenly they knew where their teammates were, passing almost by instinct, behaving, in fact, like a team.

By the final whistle the score remained the same and Max trotted to the sideline, joined in the scrum while they offered a cheer for Madison and then began picking up his gear. This was the sort of game he had always wanted to play in, he thought, and now there was a good chance he would play in several more before the summer ended. He didn't know anyone was behind him until he stood up and there was Basil standing next to a man he didn't recognize.

"Max," Basil said, "I want you to meet Mr. Tallyman. He's the soccer coach at Choate."

Tall, and blond, Mr. Tallyman looked as if he could step onto any field in the world. He stuck out his hand. "Max, it's good to meet you," he said, his accent distinctly English. "And congratulations on an excellent match."

"Nice to meet you, sir," Max said. "I can't believe I didn't stop that last one."

"Do you know why you didn't?"

"I committed too soon. I didn't think the guy would shoot from that far out when he had a guy headed for the goal."

"Quite. Yet you still made an astonishing recovery."

Max grinned. "Thanks."

"Basil tells me you might be interested in Choate."

"Well, I've been thinking about that."

"I can't make any promises about playing time, but if

you're truly interested, I'll have a talk with the admissions people."

"I don't know whether I'm smart enough," Max said.

"Why don't we worry about that later. Would you like me to talk to your parents?"

Max nodded. "That would be the best way," he said.

"When can I set up an appointment?"

"My Dad's here today. You could talk to him right now." He slung his gear bag over his shoulder. "Com'on, I'll introduce you."

They walked over to where Tom was standing with several friends.

"Dad, I want you to meet Mr. Tallyman. He's the soccer coach at Choate and he'd like to talk to you."

His father grinned and stuck out his hand. "Tom Murphy."

"Bard Tallyman."

"Basil and I will be over with the team," Max said.

When they were out of range, Max turned to Basil and grinned. "You're a sly fox, you are."

Basil shrugged. "I couldn't stand the thought of you not playing this fall. I told you. Sometimes I can't wait."

Max saw the man step from behind a tree ten feet away, but until he saw him reach for his pocket he thought nothing about it. When he did, he reacted at mongoose speed, pushing Basil clear and then rushing the guy, coming in low and very fast so by the time the pistol had cleared his pocket Max was on him, driving his head into the man's midsection so hard it pushed the air from the guy's lungs, and slammed him backward onto the ground, the pistol flying from his hand. Two FBI agents closed in a rush and Max was in their face.

"You were supposed to be protecting me! Where were you? I thought you guys were pros and instead it takes a kid to get it done!"

"Calm down, Max," the shorter of the two agents said. "Nobody can be everywhere at once."

Max was hot, his ears and his face felt as if they were on fire. "You guys were supposed to have this under control!"

While the tall agent put the cuffs on the guy, the other turned and smiled. "We did, Max. We saw him and we'd have taken him out but you got there first and then we couldn't shoot. You were too fast for us, Max. I never saw anyone move that fast."

He didn't know what to say, and finally he nodded and apologized. "All I could do was react," he said.

The agent laughed. "You're not afraid of much, are you?"

"Of course I am. I'm afraid of all kinds of things. Especially tigers. I am terrified of tigers. And bears. Tigers and bears."

He felt a hand on his arm and when he turned there was Meg.

"Are you all right?" she asked.

It was as if someone had opened a gate valve and drained away what was left of his rage. "I'm fine," he said.

She took his hand and squeezed. "I've never been so terrified. Weren't you scared?"

He shook his head. He could feel the ground under his feet again. "I just thought I didn't want to be killed today."

She laughed and squeezed his hand again and this time he squeezed back.

Eighteen

A Special Delivery

Max sat in the kitchen with a cup of coffee, looking out across the drive at the foundation for the new barn. Dad said it would be up by September, but that was only three weeks away, and every day now he grew more tense as he waited to hear from Choate. What was taking them so long to tell him they weren't accepting him? Maybe he'd been wrong when he told Basil he was good at waiting, because he wasn't very good at it. He felt like a hard rubber ball that spent its days bouncing from ceiling to floor.

But at least the hydrogen generator was working and the gas was gradually finding its way into the new cylinders. So far he had two dozen cylinders spread out over the lawn and by the time school started he ought to have at least twice that many.

He looked up as a Fed Ex truck pulled into the drive. He stood and walked out to the truck, wondering why the driver had stopped so far from the house.

He hadn't ordered anything and his parents usually

had stuff delivered to The Trap. There was definitely something wrong and though he showed no outward change, his body was on full alert as he walked over to the truck. Suddenly the door opened and he was looking into the barrel of a pistol.

"You've got something that belongs to me."

Max looked at him. "I have?"

"It was on the boat."

"What boat?"

"The one on the beach."

"I didn't take anything from the boat."

"You're the only one who could have taken it."

The tall, ugly young man stepped out of the truck and grabbed Max by his left arm, his grip strong. "We can do this the easy way, or we can do it the hard way. You saw the man on the boat. That's what happens to people who don't cooperate. Now where is it?"

Not good, Max thought, not good at all. They couldn't be seen from the road, and his cell phone was in the house. "I told you," Max said, "I didn't take anything from the boat. But I went another time and I found a metal tube in a flashlight. The FBI has it now."

"Lying is pointless. If the Feds had it they would have gone public. It would have been in the papers."

"They couldn't because the stuff on Plum is too dangerous and they didn't want anyone to know it had gotten off the island."

The grip loosened slightly and then clamped down harder. Max tried to think, to clear his head, and very slowly he drew a deep, deep breath and let it out.

"They aren't that smart," the man said. He pulled Max toward the truck. "We're going to where I've got more time to deal with you."

At first Max didn't resist and then he remembered the headless yachtsman and what they had done to him before they cut his head off. They'd pulled out his fingernails, they'd broken his legs and arms. And that's what they'd do to him. But the bottom line was that whether he talked or not, the guy would kill him in the end and that meant he had to do something and do it fast. He tried stumbling and falling to the ground, but before he got halfway down, the man snatched him back onto his feet.

The gun looked very nasty, but was he any good with it? Could he hit a moving target? Do I want to find out? The only guns he knew about were the shotguns they used for duck hunting in the fall. When it came to handguns he had to rely on what he'd seen in the movies, and he was pretty sure that wasn't real reliable. He knew one other thing. No adult expects a kid to attack. He also knew he had to get into the woods as quickly as possible because it had to be a lot harder to hit a moving target in the woods than in the open.

It meant breaking free and getting to the other side of the truck but clearly, he had to get into the woods. After all the time he'd spent in the Scouts with the Indian Chief in North Madison, he knew about the woods and he'd bet anything this was a city guy. All he needed was an opening. But the guy was strong and ... and there was no time. Once he got him into the truck he'd have no chance.

Max went for it. He let his body sag toward the ground

and then he came up and pivoted and brought his foot right up into guy's crotch feeling a sharp pain in the top of his foot. The guy was wearing a cup! Who would have expected that?

But while the cup took the edge off what would have been a disabling blow, it served to break the grip on his arm and send the guy reeling back into the truck, and Max darted around the truck and into the woods. Then he ran, dodging through the trees, trying to avoid the patches of green briar tearing at his arms and his legs.

He heard the guy curse and plunge into the woods, crashing through the brush. From behind a big tulip poplar Max peered back the way he had come. The guy was following, and he'd screwed a silencer into the large semi-automatic pistol. Worse, he was coming right down the trail Max had left in passing. Max slipped behind the tree, his mind whirling as he tried to decide on a strategy. Somewhere up ahead there was the path he had used to get to the tree fort when he was younger. It had probably grown in, but at least he could make good time.

He was also going to make plenty of noise, but right now that would work in his favor. He darted from behind the tree and ran, certain the guy wouldn't shoot him. His only chance to get the vial was to take him alive.

The big tulip poplars grew like silent giants from the forest floor and for a short way the big trees had shaded out the underbrush and then the ground grew wet and soggy underfoot and the only way past the dense witch hazel was to crash through. He cut onto the path, surprised that it had not grown in more, and now he ran as fast as he could toward the old white oak where he and Wayne had built the tree house. The giant old wolf tree had lost some branches to lightning and wind storms in the past few years but the tree house still sat in the spread of the two branches that reached outward like giant arms. Even the ladder was there, leaning against the trunk of the tree.

He could hear the guy cursing and grunting as the green briars tore at his clothes, but he kept on coming and then finally he reached the path and began trotting toward him. He was sweating hard in the humid heat that hunkered beneath the trees where the breeze couldn't pull it away.

At the base of the tree the guy stopped, looking up at the tree house. "Okay, kid. Dead end. Com'on down. You can't get away from me, but you don't have to get hurt. Either come down quietly or I start shooting. This is a big gun, kid. The bullets will go right through the wood. Now, be a nice little boy and come down before I start shooting."

At that instant the nice little boy hit the big ugly guy in the back of the neck with a rock-hard branch from the old white oak and slammed him head first into the trunk of the tree. The guy slid downward, the gun falling from his hand and then he lay absolutely still. Max grabbed the gun. It looked like any one of the guns he had seen in the movies and he tried to remember what they did to them to keep them from firing.

Safety. There had to be a safety. And then he remembered that they always let the clip out of the handle and he pushed a button and the clip fell onto the ground. The next thing they did was pull back the top of the gun, and he grabbed hold and pulled. It moved and he pulled harder and the slide came back and ejected the cartridge that had been in the chamber. He picked up the clip and the cartridge and looked down at the guy. He hadn't moved and Max wondered if he'd killed him.

For an instant he was tempted to find out and then he stepped back, turned, and ran for the house. What did it matter whether he was dead or not? It was time to get help.

He dialed the phone. "Mrs. Field, this is …"

"I know who it is, Max."

"Can you tell Uncle Carl to get up to the house right away. Some guy just tried to kill me!"

She laughed. "Okay, Max, you got my attention. But you have to understand."

While she jabbered away Max cradled the phone with his shoulder, walked out onto the back porch, unscrewed the silencer from the end of the gun, slipped the clip into the handle, ran the slide back, aimed at the ground, and, then holding the phone close by, he fired the gun. The noise and the sudden lurch and twist of the gun in his hand startled him. He put his ear to the phone. "Did you hear that, Mrs. Field? That was the gun I took away from the guy."

"My ear! Oh my God! You've ruined my hearing!"

"Use the other ear!" Max shouted.

Suddenly the phone went silent. "Max?"

"Uncle Carl?"

"What in the name of Sam Hill is going on, Max?"

"I'm at the house. Some guy just tried to kill me, but I knocked him out with a tree branch and took his gun."

"Is the gun loaded, Max?"

"Yes."

"Can you empty it?"

"Yup."

"Empty it and wait for me. I'll only be a few minutes."

"Uncle Carl?"

"Yeah?"

"I hit him pretty hard, Uncle Carl."

"I'll send the EMTs."

☞　　☞　　☞

He sat on the porch with Basil and Meg and Lord and Lady Greene. "I talked to Uncle Carl this morning and he finally gave me the whole story." He took a long swallow of Pepsi. "There was all kinds of stuff going on that nobody knew about. And until they got the guy who tried to kill me to talk, they had no idea how high it went." He looked around at Basil. "You remember the guys at Sag Harbor talking about the boss?"

Basil nodded.

"Well it turns out that he's kind of a nobody. Just a small time crook who was dealing drugs and built up enough money to try something bigger. I mean the guy was a total screw up. He hired a bunch of dummies and they kept messing up. For example, the boat wasn't supposed to go ashore. They were supposed to scuttle it after they got the vial with the germs in it from Waterstreet, but he wouldn't give it up even after they killed the woman they thought was his girlfriend. But it turned out that he hardly knew her. He'd picked her up in a bar the night before, stolen the boat and tried to make his getaway. But they had been following him. One of the guys who caught up with him was a real crazy and he got carried away and killed Waterstreet before he told them where to look for the vial. Then they panicked, set the boat on auto pilot, figuring it would run up onto the rocks and explode, and then jumped overboard and the guy who chased us picked them up. But of course they forgot to set a course for the rocks so the boat wound up on the beach.

"Waterstreet was a smuggler and he was hired by the boss to make the exchange with the guy from Plum Island. But he killed the guy, kept the money, and they think he was going to sell the vial himself.

"The funny thing is that the vial was perfectly clean. The guy in the lab hadn't given them anything more than the stuff they use in the labs to grow things. Uncle Carl says it was a pretty neat plan on the part of the guy in the lab, because the only way they could have known they didn't get anything for their money was to open the vial and they wouldn't have dared to do that."

"What about the missiles?" Basil asked.

"That was a completely different deal. They were going to a bunch of revolutionaries in Brooklyn who were planning to shoot down airliners coming out of LaGuardia."

Lord Greene smiled. "You're quite a hero, Max."

Max shook his head. "Mostly I think I'm pretty lucky." He reached for his back pocket and pulled out a letter. "Really lucky." He took the letter from the envelope and unfolded it, then handed it to Lord Greene. "Choate says I can go there in September."

"All right!" Basil shouted. "We're gonna sweep every team we play!"

Max looked at Meg and there was no mistaking the warmth in her smile as he smiled back at her. Maybe if they could just stay close friends for long enough, then maybe it would lead to something else. Or maybe not. The worst part about being a kid, Max thought, was having to wait for everything. In a way it was like a perpetual Christmas, and you could never be certain whether you'd wind up with what you wanted or a stocking full of coal. All you could do was narrow the odds.

"By the by," Lord Greene said, "it's all clear with your folks if you'd like to come back to England with us for a couple of weeks."

"Wow!" Max shouted. "That would be awesome!"

Lord Green smiled. "Actually, this has been in the works for some time. Long enough so your mother was able to get your passport."

"This is so incredible!" Max shook his head. "Thank you very much!"

"I told you," Basil said, "we'll be fishing for salmon in the Spey."

Max grinned. Suddenly he could not sit still and he popped up out of his chair. "Okay, I've got a fast boat, a full tank of gas and nearly flat water. Who wants to go skiing?"

On the way to the pier, Meg slipped her hand into his. It made him feel strong. He grinned and looked around at her. "Bob's your uncle," he said, and indeed, things could hardly have been more perfect.

About the Author

Robert Holland has a B.A. in history from the University of Connecticut and an M.A. in English from Trinity College. He studied writing under Rex Warner at UConn and under Stephen Minot at Trinity.

He has worked as a journalist, a professor, a stock broker, an editor, and from time to time anything that put food on the table. He hunts, he is a fly fisherman, a wood-carver, a cabinet maker, and he plays both classical and folk guitar.

While he was never a great athlete, he played with enthusiasm and to some extent overcame his lack of ability by teaching himself how to play and then practicing.

Sometime during college he decided he wanted to be a writer and has worked at it ever since, diverting the energy he once poured into sports to becoming not only a writer, but a writer who understands the importance of craft. Like all writers he reads constantly, not only because, as Ernest Hemingway once said, "you have to know who to beat," but because it is the only way to gather the information which every writer must have in his head, and because it is a way to learn how other writers have developed the narrative techniques which make stories readable, entertaining, and meaningful.

He lives in Woodstock, Connecticut, with his wife, Leslie, his daughter, Morgan, his son, Gardiner, and varying numbers of Labrador retrievers, cats, and chickens.